"You have plenty of reason to be worried," Sean reminded Emily.

"Don't make this into a worst-case scenario." Emily continued to hold his hand, and he felt the tension in her grip.

"Seriously, Emily, you *do* need a bodyguard."

"I agree, and the job is yours."

He'd expected an argument but was glad that she'd decided to be rational. He glanced toward the dining room. The snowstorm raged outside the windows. "I could do with another bowl of chili."

"Me, too."

Before she hopped down the step to the floor, she went up on tiptoe and gave him a kiss on the forehead. It was nothing special, the kind of small affection a wife might regularly bestow on her husband. The utter simplicity blew him away.

Before she could turn her back and skip off into the dining room, he caught her hand and gave a tug. She was in his arms. When her body pressed against his, they were joined together the way they were supposed to be.

Then he kissed her.

MOUNTAIN BLIZZARD

USA TODAY Bestselling Author

CASSIE MILES

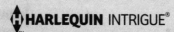

HARLEQUIN INTRIGUE®

For Nafina, who will always be my screen saver and, as always, to Rick.

Recycling programs for this product may not exist in your area.

ISBN-13: 978-0-373-75672-8

Mountain Blizzard

Copyright © 2017 by Kay Bergstrom

HARLEQUIN®

www.Harlequin.com

Printed in U.S.A.

Cassie Miles, a *USA TODAY* bestselling author, lives in Colorado. After raising two daughters and cooking tons of macaroni and cheese for her family, Cassie is trying to be more adventurous in her culinary efforts. She's discovered that almost anything tastes better with wine. When she's not plotting Harlequin Intrigue books, Cassie likes to hang out at the Denver Botanical Gardens near her high-rise home.

Books by Cassie Miles

Harlequin Intrigue

Mountain Midwife
Sovereign Sheriff
Baby Battalion
Unforgettable
Midwife Cover
Mommy Midwife
Montana Midwife
Hostage Midwife
Mountain Heiress
Snowed In
Snow Blind
Mountain Retreat
Colorado Wildfire
Mountain Bodyguard
Mountain Shelter
Mountain Blizzard

Visit the Author Profile page at Harlequin.com for more titles.

CAST OF CHARACTERS

Emily Peterson—The free-spirited poet turned investigative journalist has gotten in over her head.

Sean Timmons—Emily's ex-husband was an undercover FBI agent while they were married. Now he's her bodyguard.

"Bulldog" Barclay—A thug who works for Wynter.

Hazel Hopkins—Emily's great-aunt lives near Aspen and hires Sean to protect her niece.

Greg Levine—The FBI agent based in San Francisco is trying to help. But which side?

Doris Liu—The adoptive mother of Roger Patrone raised the boy in Chinatown.

John Morelli—Working for Wynter, his position is midlevel management, but he's only a thug.

Roger Patrone—Another Wynter employee, he lost his life trying to do the right thing.

Matt and Mason Steele—Brothers who are part of TST Security.

Jerome Strauss—The editor of a blog/newspaper who has gotten involved with the wrong people.

Dylan Timmons—Sean's brother, and a computer genius who helped found TST Security.

James Wynter—The head of a crime syndicate based in San Francisco.

Frankie Wynter—The youngest son of James Wynter is a thug, a spoiled brat and a murderer.

Lianne Zhou—A survivor of human trafficking, she is a powerful figure in Chinatown.

Mikey Zhou—The snakehead smuggler has a soft spot in his heart for his sister, Lianne.

Prologue

San Francisco
Mid-September

The double-deck luxury yacht rolled over a Pacific wave just outside San Francisco Bay as Emily Peterson wobbled down a nearly vertical staircase on her four-inch stilettos. Her short, tight, sparkly disguise gave her a new respect for the gaggle of party girls she'd hidden among to sneak on board. Somehow those ladies managed to walk on these stilts without falling and to keep their nipples covered in spite of ridiculously low-cut dresses.

Her plan for tonight was to locate James Wynter's private computer and load the data onto a flash drive. She'd slipped away from the gala birthday party for one of Wynter Corporation's top executives. The guests had been raucous as they guzzled champagne and admired their view of the Golden Gate Bridge against the night sky. Some had complained about having to surrender their cell phones, and Emily had agreed. It would have been useful to snap photos of high-ranking political types getting cozy with Wynter's thugs.

Belowdecks, she went to the second door on the right. She'd been told this was James Wynter's office. The polished brass knob turned easily in her hand. No need to pick the lock.

Pulse racing, she entered. The desk lamp was off, but moonlight through the porthole was enough to let her see the open laptop. In a matter of minutes, she could transfer Wynter's data to her flash drive, and she'd finally have the evidence she needed for her human trafficking article.

Before she reached the desk, she heard angry voices in the corridor. She backed away from the desk and ducked into a closet with a louvered door. Desperately, she prayed for them to pass by the office and go to a different room.

No such luck.

The office door crashed open. One of the men fell into the office on his hands and knees while others laughed. Another guy turned on the lamp. Light spread across the desktop and spilled onto the floor.

Her pulse thundered in her ears, but Emily stayed utterly silent. She dared not make a sound.

If Wynter's men found her, she was terrified of what they'd do.

Carefully, she stepped out of her red stilettos and went into a crouch. Through the slats in the door, she could see the shoes and legs of four men. The man who had fallen kept apologizing again and again, begging the others to believe him.

She recognized the voice of one of his tormentors: Frankie Wynter, the youngest son of James Wynter. Though she couldn't exactly tell what was going on, she thought Frankie was pushing the man who was so very sorry while the others laughed.

There was a clunk as the man who was being pushed flopped into the swivel chair behind the desk. From this angle, she saw only the back sides of the three men. One of them rocked back on his heel, cracked his knuckles and then lunged forward. She heard the slap, flesh against flesh.

They hit him again. What could she do? How could she stop them? She hated being silent while someone else suffered. Each blow made her cringe. If her ex-husband had been here, he could have made a difference, would have done the right thing. But she was on her own and utterly without backup. Should she speak up? Did she dare?

The beating stopped.

"Shut up," Frankie roared at the man in the chair. "Crying like a little girl, you make me sick."

"Let me talk. Please. I need to see the kids."

"Don't beg."

Emily saw the gleam of silver as Frankie drew his gun. Terror gripped her heart. The other two men flanked him. They murmured something about waiting for his father.

Frankie opened the center drawer on the desk and took out a silencer. "I can do what needs to be done."

"But your father—"

"He's always telling me to step up." He finished attaching the silencer to his handgun. "That's what I'm going to do."

He fired point-blank, then fired again.

When Frankie stepped away, she saw the dead man in the chair. His suit jacket was thrown open. The front of his shirt was slick with blood.

Emily pinched her lips closed to keep from crying out. She should have done something. A man was dead, and she hadn't reached out, hadn't helped him.

"We're already out at sea," Frankie said. "International waters. A good place to dump a body."

"I'll get something to carry him in."

He glanced toward the closet…

Chapter One

Colorado
Six weeks later

He'd been down this road before. Though Sean Timmons was pretty sure that he'd never actually been to Hazelwood Ranch, there was something familiar about the long, snow-packed drive bordered on either side by wood fences. He parked his cherry-red Jeep Wrangler between a snow-covered pickup truck and a snowy white lump that was the size of a four-door sedan. Peering through his windshield, he saw a large two-story house with a wraparound porch. It looked like somebody had tried to shovel his or her way out, but the wind and new snow had all but erased the path leading to the front door.

Weather forecasters had been gleefully predicting the first blizzard of the Colorado ski season, and it looked like they were right for a change. Sean was glad he wouldn't have to make the drive back to Denver tonight. He hadn't formally accepted this assignment, but he didn't see why he wouldn't.

Hazel Hopkins from Hazelwood Ranch had called his office at TST Security yesterday and said she needed a bodyguard for at least a week, possibly longer. He wouldn't be protecting Hazel but a "friend" of hers. She was vague about the threat, but he gathered that her "friend" had offended someone with a story she'd written. The situation didn't seem too dangerous. Panic words, such as *narcotics*, *crime lord* and *homicidal ax murderer*, had been absent from her conversation.

Hazel had refused to give her "friend's" name, which wasn't all that unusual. The wealthy folk who lived near Aspen were often cagey about their identities. That was okay with him. The money transfer for Hazel's retainer had cleared, and that was really all Sean needed to know. Still, he'd been curious enough to look up Hazelwood Ranch on the internet, where he'd learned that the ranch was a small operation with only twenty-five to fifty head of cattle. Hazel, the owner, was a small but healthy-looking woman with short silver hair. No clues about the identity of her "friend." If he had to guess, he'd say that the person he'd be guarding was an aging movie star who'd written one of those tell-all books and was now regretting her candor.

Soon enough he'd know the truth. He zipped his parka, slapped on a knit cap and put on heavy-duty gloves. It wasn't far to the front porch, but the snow was already higher than his ankles. Fat, wet flakes swirled around him as he left his Jeep and slogged along the remnants of a pathway to the front door.

On the porch, the Adirondack chairs and a hanging swing were covered with giant scoops of drifted snow. He stomped his boots and punched the bell under the porch lamp. Hazel Hopkins opened the door and ushered him into a warmly lighted foyer with a sweeping wrought-iron staircase and a matching chandelier with lights that glimmered like candles.

"Glad you made it, Sean." Her voice was husky. When he looked down into her lively turquoise eyes, he suspected that a lot of wild living had gone into creating her raspy tone. Though she wore jeans on the bottom, her top was kimono-style with a fire-breathing dragon embroidered on each shoulder. He had the impression that he'd met her before.

She stuck out her tiny hand. "I'm Hazel Hopkins."

Compared with hers, his hand looked as big as a grizzly bear's paw. Sean was six feet, three inches tall, and this little woman made him feel like a hulking giant.

"Hang your jacket on the rack and take off your wet boots," she said. "You're running late. It's almost dark."

"The snow slowed me down."

"I was worried."

Parallel lines creased her forehead, and he noticed that she glanced surreptitiously toward a shotgun in the corner of the entryway. Gently he asked, "Have there been threats?"

"I had a more practical concern. I was worried that you wouldn't be able to find the ranch and you couldn't reach us by phone. Something's wrong with my landline, and the blizzard is disrupting the cell phone signal."

He sat on a bench by the door to take off his wet boots.

Without pausing for breath, she continued. "You know how they always say that the weather doesn't affect your service on the cell phone or the Wi-Fi? Well, I'm here to tell you that's a lie, a bold-faced lie. Every time we have a serious snowstorm, I have a problem."

The heels on her pixie-size boots clicked on the terra-cotta floor between area rugs as she darted toward him, grabbed his boots and carried them to a drying mat under the coat hooks. She braced her fists on her hips and stared at him. "You're exactly how I remembered."

Aha, they had met before. He stood and adjusted the tail of his beige suede shirt to hide the holster he wore on his hip. "This may sound strange…" he said. "Have I ever been here?"

"I don't think so. But Hazelwood Ranch is the backdrop for many, many photos. The kids came here often."

Her explanation raised more questions. Backdrop for what? What kids? Why would he have seen the photos? "Maybe you could remind me—"

She reached up to pat his cheek. "I'm glad that you're still clean-shaven. I don't like the scruffy beard trend. I'll bet you picked up your grooming habits in the FBI."

"Plus, my mom was a good teacher."

"Not according to the photo on your TST Security website," she said. "Your brother, Dylan, has a ponytail."

"He's kind of a wild card. His specialties are electronics and cybersecurity."

"And your specialty is working with law enforcement and figuring out the crimes. I believe your third partner, Mason Steele, is what you boys call the 'muscle' in the group."

"I guess you checked me out."

"I have, indeed."

He took a long look at her, hoping to jog his brain. His mind was blank. Nothing came through. His gaze focused on her necklace, a long string of etched silver, black onyx and turquoise beads. He knew that necklace…and the matching bracelet coiled around her wrist.

Shaking his head, he inhaled deeply. A particular aroma came to him. The scent of roasted peppers, onions, chili and cinnamon mingled with honey and fresh corn bread. He couldn't explain this odor, but his lungs had been craving it. Nothing else was nearly as sweet or as spicy delicious. Nothing else would satisfy this newly awakened appetite.

His eyelids closed as a high-definition picture appeared in his mind. He saw a woman— young, fresh and beautiful. A blue jersey shift outlined her slender curves, and she'd covered the front with a ruffled white apron. Her long, sleek brown hair cascaded down her back, almost to her waist. She held a wooden spoon toward him, offering a taste of her homemade chili.

He had always wanted more than a taste. He wanted everything with her, the whole enchilada. But he couldn't have her. Their time was over.

He gazed down into her eyes…*her turquoise eyes!*

"You remember," Hazel said, "the wedding."

That Saturday in June, six and a half years ago, was a blur of color and taste and music and silence. His eyelids snapped open. "I recall the divorce a whole lot better."

These were dangerous memories, warning

bells. He should run, get the hell out of there. Instead, he followed his nose down a shadowy hallway. Stiff-legged, he marched through the dining room into the bright, warm kitchen where the aroma of chili was thick.

Two pans of golden corn bread rested near the sink on the large center island with a dark marble countertop. She stood at the stove with her back toward him, stirring a heavy cast-iron pot. She wore jeans that outlined her long legs and tight, round bottom. On top, she had on a striped sweater. Over her shoulder, she said, "Hazel, did I hear the doorbell?"

The small, silver-haired woman beside him growled a warning. "You should turn around slowly, dear."

Sean gripped the edge of the marble countertop, unsure of how he was going to feel when he faced her. Every single day since their divorce five years ago—after only a year and a half of marriage—he had imagined her. Sometimes he remembered the sweet warmth of her body beside him in their bed. Other times he saw her from afar and reveled in coming closer and closer. Usually, he imagined her naked with her dark chestnut hair spilling across her olive skin.

Her hair! He stared at her back and shoulders. She'd chopped off her lush, silky hair.

"Emily," he said.

She whirled. Clearly surprised, she wielded

her wooden spoon like a knife she might plunge into his chest. "Sean."

Her turquoise eyes were huge, outlined with thick, dark lashes. Her mouth was a thin, tight line. Her dark brows pulled down, and he immediately recognized her expression, a look he'd seen often while they were married. She was furious. What the hell did she have to be angry about? He was the one who had driven through a blizzard.

He stepped away from the counter, not needing the support. The anger surging through his veins gave him the strength of ten. "I don't know what kind of sick game you two ladies are playing, but it's not funny. I'm leaving."

"Good." She stuck out her jaw and took a step toward him. "I don't want you hanging around."

"Then why call me up here? I had a verbal contract, an agreement." TST had a strict no-refund policy, but this was a special circumstance. He'd pay back the retainer from his own pocket. "Forget it. I'll give your money back."

"What money?" Emily's upper lip curled in a sneer that she probably thought was terrifying. Yeah, right, as terrifying as a bunny wiggling its nose.

"You hired me."

"Not me." Emily threw her spoon back into the chili pot. "Aunt Hazel, what have you done?"

The silver-haired woman with dragons on her

shoulders had maneuvered her way around so she was standing at the far end of the center island with both of them on the other side. "When you two got married, I always thought you were a perfect match."

"You were the only one," Emily said.

Unfortunately, that was true. Sean and Emily were both born and raised in Colorado, but they had met in San Francisco. She was a student at University of California in Berkeley, majoring in English and appearing at least once a week at local poetry slams. At one of these open-mike events, he saw her.

She'd been dancing around on a small stage wearing a long gypsy skirt. Her wild hair was snatched up on her head with dozens of ribbons. He'd been impressed when she rhymed "appetite" and "morning light" and "coprolite," which was a technical word for fossilized poop. He would have stayed and talked to her, but he'd been undercover, rooting out a drug dealer at the slam venue. Sean had been in the FBI.

When they told people they were getting married, their opposite lifestyles—Bohemian chick versus federal agent—were the first thing people pointed to as a reason it would never work. The next issue was an age difference. She was nineteen, and he was twenty-seven. Eight years wasn't really all that much, but her youthful immaturity stood in stark contrast to his orderly, responsible lifestyle.

"If you'd asked me at the time," Aunt Hazel said, "I'd have advised you to live together before marriage."

Sean hadn't wanted to take that chance. He had hoped the bonds of marriage would help him control his butterfly. "It was a mistake," he said.

Emily responded with a snort.

"You don't think so?" he asked.

"Are you still here? You were in such a rush to get away from me."

His contrary streak kicked in. He sure as hell wasn't going to let her think that she was chasing him out the door. Very slowly and deliberately, he pulled out a stool and took a seat at the center island opposite the stove top. He turned away from Emily.

"Aunt Hazel," he said, "you still haven't told us why you hired me as a bodyguard."

"You? A bodyguard?" Emily sputtered. "You're not a fed anymore?"

"Do you care?"

"Why should I?"

"What are you doing now?" he asked.

"Writing."

"Poetry?" He scoffed.

She exhaled an eager gasp as she tilted her head and leaned toward him. Her turquoise eyes flashed. Her face, framed by wisps of brown hair, was flushed beneath the natural olive tint. He remembered her spirit and her enthusiasm, and he knew that she wanted to tell him something. The words were poised at the tip of her tongue, straining to jump out.

And he wanted to hear them. He wanted to share with her, to listen to her stories and to feel the waves of excitement that radiated from her. Emily had always thrown herself wholeheartedly into whatever she was attempting to do. It was part of her charm. No doubt she had some project that was insanely ambitious.

With a scowl, she raised her hand, palm out, to hold him away from her. "Just go."

"Such drama," Aunt Hazel said. "The two of you are impossible. It's called communication, and it's not all that difficult. Sean, you're going to sit there and I'm going to tell you what our girl has been up to."

"I don't have to listen to this," Emily said.

"If I'm not explaining properly, feel free to jump in," Hazel said. "First of all, Emily doesn't write poems anymore. After the divorce, she changed her focus to journalism."

"Totally impractical," he muttered. "With all the newspapers going out of business, nobody makes a living as a journalist."

"I do all right."

Her voice was proud, and there was a strut in her step as she strolled from one end of the island to the other. Watching her long, slender legs and the way her hips swayed was a treat. He felt himself being drawn into her orbit. She'd always had the power to mesmerize him.

"Fine," he muttered. "Tell me about your big deal success in journalism."

"Right after the divorce, I got a job writing for the *Daily Californian*, Berkeley's student newspaper. I learned investigative techniques, and I blogged. And I started doing articles for online magazines. I have a regular bimonthly piece in a national publication, and they pay very nicely."

"For articles about eye shadow and shoes?"

"Hard-hitting news." She slammed her fist on the marble island. "I witnessed a murder."

"Which is why I called you," Aunt Hazel said. "Emily's life is in danger."

This was just crazy enough to be possible. "Have you received threats?"

"Death threats," she said.

His feet were rooted to the kitchen floor. He didn't want to stay…but he couldn't leave her here unprotected.

Chapter Two

Emily couldn't look away from him. Fascinated, she watched as a muscle in Sean's jaw twitched, his brow lowered and his eyes turned as black as polished obsidian. He was outrageously masculine.

With a nearly imperceptible shrug, his muscles tensed, but his frame didn't contract. He seemed to get bigger. His fingers coiled into fists, ready to lash out. He was prepared to defend her against anything and everything. His aggressive stance told her that he'd take on an army to keep her from harm.

When she thought about it, his new occupation as a bodyguard made sense. Sean had always been a protector, whether it was keeping a bully away from his sweet-but-nerdy brother or rescuing a stray dog by stopping four lanes of traffic on a busy highway. If Sean had been hiding in that louvered closet instead of her, he would have saved the man she now could identify as Roger Patrone.

Sean reached toward her. She yanked her arm away. She didn't dare allow him to get too close. No matter how much she wanted his embrace, that wasn't going to happen. This man had been the love of her life. Ending their marriage was the most difficult thing she'd ever done, and she couldn't bear going through that soul-wrenching pain again.

"Did you report the murder to the police?" he asked.

"Of course," she said, "and to your former FBI bosses. Specifically, I had several chats with Special Agent Greg Levine. I'm surprised he didn't call and tell you."

"Levine is still stationed in San Francisco," he said. "Is that where the crime took place?"

"Yes."

"In the city?"

"Just beyond the Golden Gate Bridge."

"In open waters," he said. "A good place to dump a body."

It was a bit disturbing that his FBI-trained brain and Freddie Wynter's nefarious instincts drew exactly the same conclusion. *Maybe you need to think like a criminal to catch one.* "As it turned out, the ocean wasn't such a great dump site. The victim washed up on Baker Beach five days later."

"The waiting must have been rough on you," he said. "It's no fun to report a murder when the body goes missing."

Definitely not fun when the investigating officer was buddy-buddy with her ex-husband. She'd asked Greg not to blab to Sean, but she'd expected him to ignore her request. Those guys stuck together. The only time Sean had lied to her when they were married was when he was covering up for a fellow fed.

She wondered if Sean's departure from the FBI had been due to negative circumstances. Had Mr. Perfect screwed up? Gotten himself fired? "Why did you leave the FBI?"

"It was time."

"Cryptic," she snapped.

"It's true."

God forbid he give her a meaningful explanation! Leaving the FBI must have been traumatic for him. Sean was born to be a fed. He could have been a poster boy with his black hair neatly barbered and his chin clean-shaven and his beige chamois suede shirt looking like it had come fresh from the dry cleaner's. He'd been proud to be a special agent. Would he confide in her if they'd fired him? "You can be so damn annoying."

"Is that so?"

"I hate when you put off a perfectly rational query with a macho statement that doesn't really tell me anything, like a man's got to do what a man's got to do."

"I don't expect you to understand."

"Mission accomplished."

Hostility vibrated around him. A red flush climbed his throat. Oh yeah, he was angry. Hot and angry. They could have put him on the porch and melted the blizzard.

"I'll leave," he said.

"Not in this storm," Aunt Hazel said. "The two of you need to calm down. Have some chili. Try to be civil."

Emily stepped away from the stove, folded her arms at her waist and watched with a sidelong gaze as Sean and her aunt dished up bowls of chili and cut off slabs of corn bread. Sean managed to squash his anger and transform into a pleasant dinner guest. She could have matched his politeness with a cold veneer of her own, but she preferred to say nothing.

There had been a time—long ago when she and Sean were first dating—when she was known for her candor. Every word from her lips was truth. She had been 100 percent frank and open.

Those days were gone.

She'd glimpsed the ugliness, heard the cries of the hopeless, learned that life wasn't always good and people weren't always kind. She'd lost her innocence.

And Hazel was correct. She'd gotten herself into trouble from the Wynters. Though she didn't want to be, she was terrified. Almost anything could set off her fear…an unexpected phone call, the slam of a door, a car that followed too closely. She hadn't gotten a good night's sleep since that night in James Wynter's closet.

The only reason she hadn't disintegrated into a quivering mass of nerves was simple: Wynter and his men didn't know her identity. Her FBI contact had told her that they knew there was a witness to the murder, but didn't know who. It was only a matter of time before they found out who she was and came after her. *Tell him. Tell Sean. Let him be your bodyguard.*

Her aunt asked, "Emily, can I get you something to drink?"

Hazel and Sean had already sprinkled grated cheddar on top of their chili bowls and added a spoonful of sour cream. They were headed to the adjoining dining room.

What would it hurt to have dinner with him? The more she looked at him, the more she saw hints of his former self, her husband, the gentleman, the broad-shouldered man who had stolen her heart. She remembered the first time they were introduced when he'd tried to shake hands and she gave him a hug. They'd always been opposites and always attracted.

"I'm not hungry," Emily said.

"There's no reason to be so stubborn," Hazel scolded. "I've hired you a bodyguard. Let the man do his job."

"I don't want a bodyguard."

She glared at Sean, standing so straight and tall like a knight in shining armor. She was drawn to his strength. At the same time, he ticked her off. She wanted to tip him over like an extra-large tin can.

Edging closer to the kitchen windows, she pushed aside the curtain and peered outside. Day had faded into dusk, and the snow was coming down hard and fast. The blizzard wasn't going to let up; he'd be here all night. She'd be spending the night under the same roof with him? *This could be a problem, a big one.*

"I've got a question for you," he said as he strolled past her and set his chili bowl on a woven place mat. "What kind of murder would trigger an FBI investigation?"

"The man who pulled the trigger is Frankie Wynter."

He startled. "The son of James Wynter?"

She'd said too much. The best move now was to retreat. She stretched and yawned. "I'm tired, Aunt Hazel. I think I'll go up to my room."

Without waiting for a response, she pivoted and ran from the kitchen. In the foyer, she paused to put Hazel's rifle in the closet. It was dangerous to leave that thing out. Then she charged up the staircase, taking two steps at a time. In her bedroom, she turned on the lamp and flopped onto her back on the queen-size bed with the handmade crazy quilt.

Memory showed her the picture of Roger Patrone sprawled back in the swivel chair with his necktie askew and his shirt covered in blood. When they came toward the closet, looking for something to wrap around poor Roger, she'd expected to be the next victim. She'd held tightly to the doorknob, hoping they'd think it was locked.

There had been no need to hold the knob. Frankie told them to get the plastic shower curtain from the bathroom. Blood wouldn't seep through. His quick orders had made her think that he might have pulled this stunt before. Other bodies might have gone over the railing of his daddy's double-decker yacht. Other murders might have been committed.

She stood, lurched toward the door, pivoted and went back to the bed. Trapped in her room like a child, she had no escape from memory. Her chest tightened. It felt like a giant fist was squeezing her lungs, and she couldn't get enough oxygen. She sat up straight. She was hot and cold at the same time. Her head was dizzy. Her breath came in frantic gasps.

With a moan, she leaned forward, put her head between her knees and told herself to inhale through her nose and exhale through her mouth. Breathe deeply and slowly. Wasn't working—her throat was too tight. Was she having a panic attack? She didn't know; she'd never had this feeling before.

The door to her bedroom opened. Sean stepped inside as though he didn't need to ask her permission and had every right to be there. She would have yelled at him, but she couldn't catch her breath. Her pulse fluttered madly.

He crossed the carpet and sat beside her on the bed. His arm wrapped around her shoulders. His masculine aroma, a combination of soap, cedar forest and sweat, permeated her senses as she leaned her head against his shoulder.

Her hands clutched in a knot against her breast, but she felt her heart rate beginning to slow down. She was regaining control of herself. Somehow she'd find a way to handle the fear. And she'd set things right.

Gently, he rocked back and forth. "Better?"

"Much." She took a huge gulp of air.

"Do you want to talk about what happened?"

"I already did. I told your buddy, Agent Levine."

"Number one, he's not my buddy. Number two, why didn't he offer to put you in witness protection?"

"I turned it down," she said.

"Emily, do you know how dangerous Frankie Wynter is?"

"I've been researching Wynter Corp for over a year," she said. "Their smuggling operations, gambling and money laundering are nasty crimes, but the real evil comes from human trafficking. Last year, the port authorities seized a boxcar container with over seventy women and children crammed inside. Twelve were dead."

"And Wynter Corp managed to wriggle out from under the charges."

"The paperwork vanished." That was one of the bits of evidence she'd hoped to get from James Wynter's computer. "There was no indication of the sender or the destination where these people were to be delivered. All they could say was that they were promised jobs."

"This kind of investigation is best left to the cops."

She separated from him and rose to her feet. "I know what I'm doing."

"I'm not discounting your ability," he said. "You might be the best investigative reporter of all time, but you don't have the contacts. Not like the FBI. They've got undercover people everywhere. Not to mention their access to advanced weaponry and surveillance equipment."

"I understand all that." He wasn't telling her anything she hadn't already figured out for herself.

"You're a witness to a crime. That's it—that's all she wrote."

She braced herself against the dresser and looked into the large mirror on the wall. Her reflection showed her fear in the tension around her eyes and her blanched complexion. Sean—ever the opposite—seemed calm and balanced.

"Can I tell you the truth?" she asked.

"That would be best."

She made eye contact with his reflection in the mirror. "I didn't actually witness the shooting. I saw Frankie with the gun in his hand. He screwed on a silencer. I heard the gunshot, and I saw the bullet holes…and the blood. But I didn't actually witness Frankie pointing the gun and pulling the trigger."

"Minor point," he said. "A good prosecutor can connect those dots."

"The body that washed ashore five days later was too badly nibbled by fishes for identification." She splayed her fingers on the dresser and stared down at them. "I was kind of hoping he was someone else, someone who jumped off the Golden Gate Bridge, but Agent Levine matched his DNA."

"To what?"

"I'd given a description to a sketch artist and identified the victim from a mug sheet photo. His name was Roger Patrone."

He shrugged. "I don't know him."

"He was thirty-five, only a couple of years older than you, and made his living with a small-time gambling operation in a cheesy strip joint. Convicted of fraud, he served three years."

"You've done your homework."

"Never married, no kids, he was orphaned when he was nine and grew up with a family in Chinatown. He speaks the language, eats the food, knows the customs and has a reputation as a negotiator for Wynter."

"Roger sounds like a useful individual," Sean said. "I'm guessing the old man wasn't too happy about this murder."

"Yeah, well, blood is still thicker than water. The FBI brought Frankie in for questioning, but one of the other guys in Wynter Corp confessed to killing Patrone and claimed self-defense. He took the fall for the boss's son."

Sean left the bed and came up behind her. His chest wasn't actually touching her back, but if she moved one step, she'd be in his arms.

In a measured tone, he said, "You're telling me that Frankie's not in custody."

"No, he's not."

"And he knows there's a witness."

"Yes."

"Did you write about the murder?"

"Agent Levine asked me not to." But she had written many articles about the evil-doing of Wynter Corporation.

"Does Frankie have your name?"

"No," she said. "I write under an alias, three

different aliases, in fact. And I have two dummy blogs. Since my communication with these publications is via the internet, nobody even knows what I look like."

"Smart."

"Thank you." Her reflection smiled at his. *So far, so good.* She might make it through the night with no more explanation than that. There was more to tell, but she didn't want to get involved with Sean. Not again.

He continued. "And you're also smart to have left Frankie and the other thugs behind in San Francisco. Hazelwood Ranch seems like a safe place to stay until this all dies down."

Unfortunately, she hadn't come to visit Aunt Hazel for safety reasons. Her gaze flickered across the surface of the mirror. She didn't want to tell him.

He leaned closer, whispered in her ear. "What is it, Emily? What do you want to say?"

The words came tumbling out. "Frankie is here in Colorado. The Wynter family has a gated compound over near Aspen. I didn't come here to give up on my investigation. I need to go deeper."

He grasped her upper arms. "Leave this to the police."

From downstairs, there was a scream.

Chapter Three

"Aunt Hazel!"

Though Emily's immediate reaction was to run toward the sound of the scream, Sean only allowed her to take two steps before he grabbed her around the middle and yanked her so hard that her feet left the floor. This was why he'd been hired.

He dragged her across the bedroom. There was only one thought in his mind: get her to safety. In the attached bathroom, he set her down beside a claw-foot tub.

"Stay here," he ordered as he drew his gun. "Keep quiet."

"The hell I will."

Though he hated to waste time with explanation, she needed to know what was going on. He spoke in a no-nonsense tone. "If there's been a break-in, they're after you. If you turn yourself in, we have no leverage. For your Aunt Hazel's safety, you need to avoid being taken captive."

"Okay, help her." Her face flushed red with fear and anger. Her eyes were wild. She pushed at his shoulder with both hands. "Hurry!"

Moving fast, he crossed to her closed bedroom door. He wished he was wearing boots instead of just socks. If he had to go outside, his feet would turn to ice. He paused at the door and mentally ran through the layout of the house. From the upstairs landing, he could see the front door. He'd know if someone had broken in that way.

Sean was confident in his ability to handle one intruder, maybe two. But Frankie Wynter had a lot of thugs at his disposal, and they were loyal; one guy was willing to face a murder rap for the boss's son. One—or two or more—of them might be standing outside her bedroom door right now.

But he didn't hear anything. Outside, the snow rattled against the windows. The wind whistled. From downstairs, he heard shuffling noises. A heavy fist rapping at the door? A muffled shout. Sean turned the knob, pulled the door open and braced the gun in his hands, ready to shoot.

There was no one on the upstairs landing.

Emily dashed to his side. "Let me help. Please!"

He'd told her to stay back and she chose to

ignore him. Emily was turning into a problem. "Is that tub in the bathroom made of cast iron?"

"It's antique. Now is not the time for a home tour."

"Get inside the tub and stay there." At least, she wouldn't be hit by a stray bullet.

"I'm coming with you."

Was she trying to drive him crazy or was this stubborn, infuriating behavior just a part of her natural personality? He couldn't exactly remember. He'd had damn good reasons for divorcing this woman. "No time to argue. Just accept the fact that I know what I'm doing."

"I need a gun."

"What you need is to listen to me."

"Please, Sean! You always carry two guns. Give one to me."

He pulled the Glock from his ankle holster and slapped it into her hand. "Do you remember how to use this?"

She recited the rules he'd taught her one golden afternoon six years ago in Big Sur. "Aim and don't close my eyes. No traditional safety on a Glock, so keep my finger off the trigger until I'm ready. Squeeze—don't yank."

"You've got the basics."

He'd treated their lessons like a game and had never insisted that she take his weapon from the combination safe when he was on assignment and she was alone at home. While he was working undercover, he'd worried about her safety, worried that she'd be hurt and it would be his fault. There was a strange irony in the fact that she'd put herself in ten times more danger than he could imagine.

He peered through the open bedroom door onto the upstairs landing where an overhead light shone down on the southwestern decor that dominated the house: a Navajo rug, a rugged side table and a cactus in an earthenware pot. A long hallway led to other bedrooms. The front edge of the landing was a graceful black wrought-iron staircase overlooking the foyer and chandelier by the front door.

Sean peered over the railing.

A menacing silence rose to greet him. He didn't like the way this was going. Emily's aunt wasn't the type of woman who cowered in silence. He gestured for Emily to stay upstairs while he descended.

At the foot of the staircase, he caught a glimpse of flying kimono dragons when Hazel raced across the foyer and skidded to a stop right in front of him.

She glared. "Where the heck is my rifle?"

Looking down from the landing, Emily said, "I moved it to the front closet."

"I had my gun right by the door," she said to Sean. "Emily shouldn't have moved it. Out of sight, out of mind."

The women in this family simply didn't grasp what it took to be cautious and safe. They needed ten bodyguards apiece. He rushed Hazel up the stairs, where she hugged Emily. The two of them commiserated as though the threat were over and done with. Had they forgotten that there might be an intruder?

"Hazel," he barked, "why did you scream?"

"I heard something outside and looked through the window. A fat lot of good it did, the snow's coming down so hard I couldn't see ten feet. But I caught a glimmer…headlights. I went toward the front door for a better look. At the exact same time, I heard somebody crashing against the back door like they were trying to bust it down. That's when I screamed."

Sean figured that five minutes had passed since they'd heard Hazel's cry for help. "After you screamed, what did you do?"

"I hid."

"Smart," he said. "You didn't reveal your hiding spot until you saw me."

She nodded, and her short silver hair bounced.

"Did you see the intruder? Did he make a noise? Was there more than one?"

"Well, my hearing isn't what it once was, but I'm pretty sure there was only one voice. And I guarantee that nobody made enough noise to tear down the back door."

As Sean herded Emily and her aunt into

Emily's bedroom, he tallied up the possible ways to break into the house. In addition to front and back door and many windows, there was likely an entrance to a root cellar or basement. The best way to limit access to the two women was to keep them upstairs. Unfortunately, it also meant they had no escape.

From Emily's bedroom, he peered through the window to the area where the cars were parked. He squinted. "I can see the outline of a truck."

"So?"

"Do you recognize it?" *Is that Frankie Wynter's truck?*

"We're in the mountains, Sean. Every other person drives a truck."

A coating of snow had already covered the truck bed; he couldn't tell if anybody had been riding in back. But the vehicle showed that someone else was on the property, even if there hadn't been other noises from downstairs.

He gave Emily a tight smile. "Stay here with Hazel. Take care of her."

"What are you going to do?"

"I'll check the doors and other points of access."

Her terse nod was a match for his smile. They were both putting on brave faces and tamping down the kind of tension that might cause your hand to tremble or your teeth to chatter. When she rested her hand against his chest, he was reminded of the early days in their marriage when she'd say goodbye before he left on assignment.

"Be careful, Sean."

He tore his gaze away from her turquoise eyes and her rose petal lips. Her trust made him feel strong and brave, even if he wasn't facing a real dragon. He was girding his loins, like a knight protecting his castle. In the old days, they would have kissed.

"I should come with you," Aunt Hazel said. "You need someone to watch your six."

"Stay here," he growled.

Emily hooked her arm around her aunt's waist. "We might as well do what he says. Sean can be a teensy bit rigid when it comes to obeying orders."

"My, my, my." Hazel adjusted the embroidered dragons on her shoulders. "Isn't that just like a fed?"

Hey, lady, you're the one who called me. And he was done playing their games. As far as he was concerned, they'd had their last warning. He refused to stand here and explain again why they shouldn't throw themselves into the line of fire when there was a possible intruder. He made a quick pivot and descended the staircase with the intention of searching the main floor.

The house was large but not so massive that he'd get lost. First, he would determine if an intruder was inside. The front door hadn't been opened. The door to a long, barrack-type wing where ranch hands might sleep during a busy season was locked, and the same was true for the basement door and the back door that opened onto a wide porch. Though it had a dead bolt, the back door lock was flimsy, easily blasted through with a couple of gunshots. As far as he could tell, no weapons had been fired.

When he pushed open the back door, a torrent of glistening snow swept inside. The area near the rear porch was trampled with many prints in the snow. Was it one person or several? He couldn't tell, but Hazel's story was true. She'd heard someone back here.

As he closed the rear door and relocked it, he heard Emily call his name. Her voice was steady, strong and unafraid. Weapon raised, he rushed toward the front of the house. The door was opening. A man in a brown parka with fur around the hood plodded inside.

Though he didn't look like much of a threat, Sean wasn't taking any chances. "Freeze."

"I sure as hell will if I don't close this door."

As the man in the parka turned to shut the front door, Hazel came down the staircase. "It's okay, Sean. This is my neighbor, Willis. He was a deputy sheriff until he retired a couple of years ago."

"I was worried, Hazel." As he shoved off his hood, unzipped the parka and stomped his snow-mobile boots, puddles of melted snow appeared on the terra-cotta tile floor. "Couldn't reach you on the phone, so I decided to come over here and check before I went to bed. Hi, Emily."

"Hey, Willis."

"Take off those boots." Hazel pointed to the bench by the door. "Are you hungry? Emily made a big pot of chili."

He sat and grinned at Sean and Emily. His face was ruddy and wet. A few errant flakes of snow still clung to his thick mustache. "And who's this young fella with the Glock?"

"Sean Timmons of TST Security." He shook the older man's meaty hand. "I'm Emily's bodyguard."

Willis was clearly intrigued. Why did Emily need protection? What other kind of security work did Sean do? He pushed the strands of wet gray hair off his forehead and straightened his mustache before he asked, "You hiring?"

"Part time," Sean said. "I can always use a man with experience as a deputy sheriff."

"Seventeen years," Willis said. "And I still work with the volunteer fire brigade and mountain search and rescue."

"Plus you've got your own little neighborhood watch." Sean had the feeling that Hazel got more attention from the retired deputy than the others in this area. "You have a key to the front door."

"That's right."

"Do you mind telling me why you banged on the back door and didn't let yourself in?"

"The back door is always unlocked, and it was a few less steps through the blizzard than the front. When I found it locked, I was pretty damn mad. I yanked at the handle to make sure it wasn't just stuck, and I might have let out a few choice swear words."

"Scared me half to death," Hazel said.

"I heard you scream." Willis looked down at the floor between his boots. He wore two pairs of wool socks. Both had seen better days. "And I felt like a jackass for scaring you."

She patted his cheek, halfway chiding and halfway flirting. "You're lucky I couldn't find my rifle."

While he explained that his keys were in the truck, and he had to tromp back out there to find the right ones, Hazel fussed over him. She was a touchy-feely person who hugged and patted and stroked. Sean noted her behavior and realized how similar it was to methods Emily used to calm him, mesmerize him and convince him to do whatever she wanted.

He glanced toward her. She sat on the fourth step, where she had a clear view of the others in the foyer. Her gaze flicked to the left, but he knew she'd been watching him. A hard woman to figure out. Was she angry or nervous? Independent or lonely?

Earlier tonight, she'd been on the verge of a panic attack. Her eyes had been wide with fear. Her muscles were so tightly clenched that she couldn't move, couldn't breathe. Scared to death, and he didn't blame her. James Wynter and his associates were undeniably dangerous.

A muscle in his jaw clenched. Why had she chosen to go after these violent criminals? And how did Levine justify leaving this witness unprotected? The FBI had been chasing Wynter for years, way before Sean was stationed in San Francisco. A chance to lock up Frankie Wynter would be a coup.

"Then it's settled," Hazel said. "Willis is sticking around for some chili and a couple of beers. You kids come into the dining room and join us."

"In a minute," Emily promised as she rose to her feet and motioned for Sean to come toward her.

She stayed on the first step, and he stood below her. They were almost eye level.

He asked, "Did you have something you wanted to say?"

"You did good tonight. I know that Hazel and I can be a handful, but you managed us. You were organized, quick. And when we thought we needed you, there you were, charging around the corner and yelling for Willis to freeze. You were…" She exhaled a sigh. "Impressive."

Her compliment made him leery. "It's what I do."

"Not that we actually needed your bodyguard skills." She caught hold of his hand and gave a squeeze. "This was a simple misunderstanding because of the blizzard."

"You have plenty of reason to be worried," he reminded her. "You mentioned the Wynter family compound near Aspen. Tonight it was Willis at the door. Tomorrow it might be Frankie Wynter."

"Don't make this into a worst-case scenario." She continued to hold his hand, and he felt the tension in her grip. "Tonight a neighbor came to pay a visit. That's all. And the blizzard is just snow. It's harmless. Kids play in it. Ever build a snowman?"

"Ever get caught in an avalanche?" He was keeping the tone light, but there was something important he needed to say. "Seriously, Emily, you need a bodyguard."

"I agree, and the job is yours."

He'd expected an argument but was glad that she'd decided to be rational. He glanced toward the dining room. "I could do with another bowl of chili."

"Me, too."

Before she hopped down the stair step to the floor, she went up on tiptoe and gave him a kiss on the forehead. It was nothing special, the kind of small affection a wife might regularly bestow on her husband. The utter simplicity blew him away.

Before she could turn her back and skip off into the dining room, he caught her hand and gave a tug. She was in his arms. When her body pressed against his, they were joined together the way they were supposed to be.

Then he kissed her.

Chapter Four

Emily hadn't intended to seduce him. That little kiss on his forehead was meant to be friendly. If she'd known she was lighting the fuse to a passionate response, she never would have gotten within ten feet of him. *Not true. I'm lying to myself.* From the moment she'd seen him, sensual memories had been taunting from the back of her mind. It was only a matter of time before that undercurrent would become manifest.

Their marriage was over, but she never had stopped imagining Sean as her lover. Nobody kissed her the way he did. The pressure of his mouth against hers was familiar and perfect. *Will he do that thing with his tongue? The thing where he parts my lips gently, and then he deepens the kiss. His tongue swoops and swirls. And there's a growling noise from the back of his throat, a vibration.*

She'd never been able to fully describe what

he did to her and what sensations he unleashed. But he was doing it right now, right in this moment. *Oh yes, kiss me again.*

She almost swooned. *Swoon? No way!* She'd changed. No more the lady poet, she was a hard-bitten journalist, not the type of woman who collapsed in a dead faint after one kiss, definitely not.

But her grip on consciousness was slipping fast. Her knees began to buckle, and she clung to his shoulders to keep from slipping to the floor. Her hands slid down his chest. Even that move was sexy; through the smooth fabric of his beige chamois shirt, she fondled his hard but supple abs.

This out-of-control but very pleasurable attraction had to stop before she lost her willpower, her rationality…her very mind. Pushing with the flat of her palms against his chest, she forced a distance between them. "We can't do this."

"Sure we can." He slung his arm around her waist. "It's been a while, but I haven't forgotten how."

Tomorrow he'd thank her for not dissolving into a quivering blob of lust. Firmly, she said, "I can see that we're going to need ground rules."

He kissed the top of her head and took a step back. "You cut it."

"What?"

"Your hair, you cut it."

"Too much trouble." She fluffed her chin-length bob. "And getting rid of the Rapunzel curls makes me look more adult."

"Oh yeah, you're really grown up. How old are you now, twenty-one? Twenty-two?"

She didn't laugh at his lame attempt at humor. "I'm almost twenty-six."

Their eight-year age difference had always been an issue. When they first met, she'd just turned nineteen. They were married and divorced before she was twenty-one, and she'd always wondered if their relationship would have lasted longer if she'd been more mature. It was a familiar refrain. *If I knew then what I know now, things would be different.*

More likely, they never would have gotten together in the first place. Older and wiser, she would have taken one look at him and realized that he wasn't the sort of man who should be married.

"I like your new haircut," he said. "And you're right. We need some ground rules."

She gestured toward the dining room. "Should we eat chili while we talk?"

"That depends on how much you want your aunt and former deputy Willis to know."

Of course, he was right. She didn't want to spill potentially dangerous information about Wynter Corp into a casual conversation. Until now the only thing she'd told Aunt Hazel was that she'd witnessed a murder in San Francisco. She hadn't named the killer or the victim and certainly hadn't mentioned that the Wynter family had a place near Aspen.

Regret trickled through her. She probably shouldn't have come here. Though she'd been ultracautious in keeping her identity secret and her connection to Hazel was hard to trace, somebody might find out and come after them. If anything happened to Hazel…

Emily shuddered at the thought. "I don't want my aunt to get stuck in the middle of this."

"Agreed."

"Come with me."

She led him across the foyer to a living room that reflected Hazel's eclectic personality with a combination of classy and rustic. The terracotta floor and soft southwestern colors blended with painted barn wood on the walls. The high ceiling was open beam. The rugged, moss rock fireplace reminded Emily that her aunt was an outdoorswoman who herded cattle and tamed wild mustangs. But Hazel also had a small art collection, including two Georgia O'Keeffe watercolor paintings of flowers that hung on either side of the fireplace.

While Emily went behind the wet bar at the far end of the room, Sean studied the watercolor of a glowing pink-and-gold hydrangea. "Is this an original?"

"A gift from the artist," Emily said. "Hazel spent some time with O'Keeffe at Ghost Ranch in New Mexico."

"I keep forgetting how rich your family is. None of you are showy. It's all casual and comfortable and then I realize that you've got valuable artwork on the wall." He made his way across the room to the wet bar. "When I was driving up to this place, I had the feeling I'd seen it before. Did we come here for a visit?"

"I don't think so. Hazel was in Europe for most of the year and a half we were married." She peered through the glass door of the wine cellar refrigerator. "White wine or red?"

"How about beer?"

"You haven't changed." She opened the under-the-counter refrigerator and selected two bottles of craft beers with zombies on the labels. "You'll like this brand. It's dark."

He didn't question her selection, just grabbed the beer, tapped the neck against hers and took a swig. He licked his lips. "Good."

A dab of foam glistened at the corner of his mouth, and she was tempted to wipe the moisture off, better yet, to lick it.

"Ground rules," she said, reminding herself as much as him.

"First, I want to know why I have déjà vu

about Hazelwood Ranch. Do you have any photo albums?"

She came out from behind the bar and shot him a glare. "If you don't mind, I'd rather not take a side trip down memory lane. We have more urgent concerns."

"You're the one who introduced family into the picture," he said. "I want to understand a few things about Hazel. How long has she lived here?"

"The ranch doesn't belong to our family. Hazel's late husband was the owner of this and many other properties near Aspen. He renamed this small ranch Hazelwood in honor of her. They always seemed so happy. Never had kids, though. He was older, in his fifties, when they got married."

She scanned the spines of books in a built-in shelf until she found a couple of photo albums. As she took them down and carried them to the coffee table in front of the sofa, she realized that she hadn't downloaded her own photos in months. Digital albums were nice, but she really preferred the old-fashioned way.

"I knew there'd be pictures," he said.

"Do you remember those journals I used to make? I'd take an old book with an interesting cover and replace the pages with my own sketches and poetry and photos."

"I remember." His voice was as soft as a caress. "The Engagement Journal was the best present you ever gave me."

"What about the watch, the super-expensive, engraved wristwatch?"

"Also treasured."

She went back to the bar, snatched up her beer and returned to sit on the sofa beside him. "I'm an excellent present giver. It's a family trait."

"How are they, the Peterson family?"

"My oldest sister had a baby girl, which means I'm an aunt, and the other two are in grad school. Mom and Dad moved to Arizona, which they love." She took a taste of the zombie beer, which was, as she'd expected, excellent, and gave him a rueful smile. "I don't suppose Aunt Hazel told my mom that she was calling you."

"Your mom hated me."

Emily made a halfhearted attempt to downplay her mother's opinion. "You weren't their favorite."

Her parents had begged her to stay in college and wait to get married until she was older. Emily was her mom's baby, the youngest of four girls, the artistic one. When Emily's divorce came, Mom couldn't wait to say "I told you so."

"Toward the end," he said, "I thought she was beginning to come around."

"It was never about you personally," she said. "I was too young, and you were too old. And

Mom didn't really like that you did dangerous undercover work in the FBI."

"And what does she think of your current profession?"

She took a long swallow of the dark beer. "Hates it."

"Does she know about the murder?"

"Oh God, no." She cringed. If her mother suspected that she was actually in danger, she'd have a fit.

Emily opened the older of the two albums. The photographs were arranged in chronological order with Emily and her sisters starting out small and getting bigger as they aged. Nostalgia welled up inside her. The Petersons were a good-looking family, wholesome and happy. In spite of what Sean thought, they weren't really rich. Sure, they had enough money to live well and take vacations and pay for school tuitions. But they weren't big spenders, and their home in an upscale urban neighborhood in Denver wasn't ostentatious.

Like her older sisters, she had tried to be what her parents wanted. They valued education, and when she told them she was considering becoming a teacher, they were thrilled. But Emily went to UC Berkeley and strayed from the path. She was a poet, a performance artist, an activist and a photographer. Her marriage and divorce to Sean had been just one more detour from the straight and narrow.

Aunt Hazel was more indulgent of Emily's free-spirited choices. Hazel approved of Sean. She'd invited him to be a bodyguard. Maybe she knew something Emily hadn't yet learned.

He stopped her hand as she was about to turn a page in the album. He pointed to a winter-time photo of her, wearing a white knit hat with a pom-pom and standing at the gate that separated Hazelwood Ranch from public lands. She couldn't have been more than five or six. Bundled up in her parka and jeans and boots, she appeared to be dancing with both hands in the air.

"This picture," he said. "You put a copy of this in the journal you gave me. I must have looked at it a hundred times. I never really noticed the outline of the hills and the curve in the road, but my subconscious must have absorbed the details. Seeing that photo is like being here."

His déjà vu was explained.

She asked, "What are we going to do to protect Hazel?"

"How does she feel about Willis? Do they have a little something going on?"

She and her aunt hadn't directly talked about who Hazel was dating, but Emily couldn't help noticing that Willis had stopped by for a visit every day. Sometimes twice a day. "Why do you ask?"

"We could hire Willis to be a bodyguard for Hazel. They might enjoy an excuse to spend more time together."

"That's not a bad idea," she said. "His performance tonight—tromping around in the snow looking for a house key—wasn't typical. Usually he's competent."

"I wouldn't want to throw him up against an army of thugs with automatic pistols," he said, "but that shouldn't be necessary. If you settle here and keep a low profile, there's no reason for Wynter to track you down. You're sure he doesn't know you're the witness?"

"I was careful, bought my plane tickets under a fake name, blocked and locked everything on my computer, threw away my phone so I couldn't be tracked."

"How did you learn to do all that?"

"Internet," she said. "I read a couple of how-to articles on disappearing yourself. Plus, I might have picked up a couple of hints when we were married."

"But you didn't like my undercover work." He leaned back against the sofa pillows and sipped his beer. "You said when I took on a new identity, it was a lie."

At the time, she hadn't considered her criticism to be unreasonable. Any new bride would be upset if her husband said he was going to be out of touch for a week or two and couldn't tell her where he was going or what he was doing. She jabbed an accusing finger in his direction. "I had every right to interrogate you, every right to be angry when you wouldn't tell me what was going on."

His dark eyes narrowed, but he didn't look menacing. He was too handsome. "You could have just trusted me."

"Trust you? I hardly knew you."

"You were my wife."

It hadn't taken long for them to jump into old arguments. Was he purposely trying to provoke her? First he mentioned the age thing. Now he was playing the "trust me" card. Damn it, she didn't want to open old wounds. "Could we keep our focus on the present? Please?"

"Fine with me." He stretched out his long legs and rested his stocking feet on the coffee table. "You claim to have covered your tracks when you traveled and when you masked your identity."

"Claimed?" Her anger sparked.

"Can you prove that you're untraceable? Can anybody vouch for you?"

"Certainly not. The point of hiding my identity is to eliminate contacts."

"Just to be sure," he said, "I'll ask Dylan to do a computer search. If anybody can hack your identity or files, he can."

"It's not necessary, but go ahead." She was totally confident in her abilities. "I've always liked your brother. How's he doing?"

"We keep him busy at TST doing computer stuff. You'll be shocked to hear that he's finally found a girlfriend who's as smart as he is. She's a neurosurgeon."

"I'm not surprised." The two brothers made a complementary pairing: Dylan was a genius, and Sean had street smarts.

"I'll use my FBI contacts, namely, Levine, to keep tabs on their investigation." He drained his beer and stood. "That should just about cover it."

"Cover what?"

"Ground rules," Sean said as he crossed the room toward the wet bar. "You and Hazel will be safe if you stay here and don't communicate with anybody. I'll need to take your cell phone."

"Not necessary," she said. "I'm aware that cell phones can be hacked and tracked. I only use untraceable burner phones."

"What about your computer?"

She swallowed hard. In the back of her mind, she knew her computer could be hacked long distance and used to track her down. There was no way she'd give up her computer. "All my documents are copied onto a flash drive."

"I need to disable the computer. No calling except on burner phones. No texting. No email. No meetings."

Anger and frustration bubbled up inside her.

Though she hadn't finished her beer and didn't need a replacement, she followed him to the bar. She climbed up on a stool and peered down at him while he looked into the under-the-counter fridge. When he stood, she glared until he met her gaze.

To his credit, Sean didn't back down, even though she felt like she was shooting lightning bolts through her eye sockets. When she opened her mouth to speak, she was angry enough to breathe fire. "Your ground rules don't work for me."

He opened another zombie beer. "What's the problem?"

"If I can't use the internet, how can I work?"

"Dylan can probably hook up some kind of secure channel to communicate with your employer."

"What if I don't want to stay here?"

"I suppose I could move you to a safe house or hotel." He came around the bar and faced her. "What's really going on?"

"Nothing."

"You always said you hated lying and liars, but you're not leveling with me. If you don't tell me everything, I can't do my job."

The real, honest-to-God problem was simple: she hadn't given up on the Wynter investigation. One of the specific reasons she'd come to Colorado was to dig up evidence against Frankie.

She swiveled around on the bar stool so she was facing away from him. "I don't want to bury my head in the sand."

"Explain."

"I want to know why Roger Patrone was murdered. And I want to stop the human trafficking from Asia."

He nodded. "We all want that."

"But I have leads to track down. If I could hook up with people from the Wynter compound and question them, I might get answers. Or I could break in and download the information on their computers. I might find evidence that would be useful to the FBI."

"Seriously?" He was skeptical. "You want to keep digging up dirt, poking the dragon?"

She shot back. "Well, that's what an investigative reporter does."

"This isn't a joke, Emily. You saw what happens to people who cross Frankie Wynter."

"They get shot and dumped."

Wynter's men could toss her body into a mountain cave, and she wouldn't be found for years. When she voiced her plan out loud, it sounded ridiculous. How could she expect to succeed in her investigation when the FBI had failed?

"If you want to take that kind of risk," he said, "that's your choice. But don't put Hazel in danger."

He was right. She shouldn't have come here,

and she definitely shouldn't have talked to him. *Trust me? Fat chance.*

Their connection had already begun to unravel, which was probably for the best. He irritated her more than a mohair sweater on a sunny day. Her unwarranted attraction to him was a huge distraction from her work. She should tell him to go. She didn't need a bodyguard.

But Sean was strong and quick, well trained in assault and protection. He knew things about investigating and undercover work that she could only guess about. Her gut instincts told her she really did need him.

"Come with me," she said. "Back to San Francisco."

Chapter Five

At five o'clock the next morning, Sean stood at the window in the kitchen and opened the blinds so he could see outside while he was waiting for the coffeemaker to do its thing. He'd turned off the overhead light, and the cool blue shadows in the kitchen melted into the shimmer of moonlight off the unbroken snow. The blizzard had ended.

Soon the phones would be working. Lines of communication would be open. There would be nothing to block Emily's return trip to San Francisco. She'd decided that she needed to go back and dig into her investigation, and it didn't look like she was going to budge.

It was up to him whether he'd go with her as her bodyguard or not. His first reaction was to refuse. She had neither the resources nor the experience to delve into the criminal depths of Wynter Corp, and she was going to get into trouble, possibly lethal trouble. He needed to make her understand her limitations without insulting her skills.

Outside, the bare branches of aspen and fir trees bent and wavered in the wind. So cold. So lonely. A shiver went through him. Their divorce had been five years ago. He should be over it. But no. He missed her every single day. Seeing her again and hearing her voice, even if she was arguing with him most of the time, touched a part of him that he kept buried.

He still cared about Emily. Damn it, he couldn't let her go to California by herself. She needed protection, and nobody could keep her safe the way he could. He would die for her... but he preferred not to.

After she'd made her announcement in the living room, she outlined the plan. "Tomorrow morning, we'll catch a plane and be in San Francisco before late afternoon. There'll be time for you to have a little chat with Agent Levine and the other guys in that office. We'll talk to my contacts on the day after that."

He'd objected, as any sane person would, but she'd already made up her mind. She flounced into the dining room and ate chili with Hazel and Willis. The prime topic of their conversation being big snowstorms and their aftermath. The chat ended with Emily's announcement that she'd be going back to San Francisco as soon as the snow stopped because she had to get back to work.

During the night, he'd gone into her room to try talking sense into her. Before he could speak, she asked if he would accompany her. When he said no, she told him to leave.

Stubborn! How could a woman who looked so soft and gentle be so obstinate? She was like a rosebush with roots planted deep—so strong and deep that she could halt the forward progress of a tank. How could he make her see reason? What sort of story could he tell her?

Finally, the coffeemaker was done. He poured a cup, straight black, for himself and one for her with a dash of milk, no sugar. Up the staircase, he was careful not to spill over the edge of the mugs. Twisting the doorknob on her bedroom took some maneuvering, but he got it open and slipped inside.

For a long moment, he stood there, watching her sleep in the dim light that penetrated around the edges of the blinds. A pale blue comforter was tucked up to her chin. Wisps of dark hair swept across on her forehead. Her eyelashes made thick, dark crescents above her cheekbones, and her lips parted slightly. She was even more beautiful now than when they were married.

She claimed that she'd changed, and he recognized the difference in some ways. She was tougher, more direct. When he thought about her rationale for investigating, he understood that she was asserting herself and building her career. Those practical concerns were in addition to the moral issues, like that need to get justice for the guy who was murdered and to right the wrongs committed by Wynter Corp. He crossed the room, placed the mugs on the bedside table and sat on the edge of her bed.

Slowly, she opened her eyes. "Has it stopped snowing?"

He nodded.

"Have you changed your mind?"

"Have you?"

She wiggled around until she was sitting up, still keeping the comforter wrapped around her like a droopy cocoon. Fumbling in the nearly dark room, she turned on her bedside lamp and reached for the coffee. "I'd like a nip of caffeine before we start arguing again."

"No need to argue. I want to help with your investigation."

"I'd be a fool to turn you down."

Damn right, you would. His qualifications were outstanding. In addition to the FBI training at Quantico, he'd taken several workshops and classes on profiling. When he first signed on, his goal was to join the Behavioral Analysis Unit. But that was not to be. His psych tests showed that his traits were better suited to a different position. He was a natural for undercover work; namely, he had an innate ability to lie convincingly.

"Plus, I'm offering the services of my brother, the computer genius and hacker."

Suspicion flickered in her greenish-blue eyes. "I appreciate the offer, but what's the quid pro quo?"

"Listen to you." He grinned. "Awake for only a couple of minutes and already speaking Latin."

She turned to look at the clock and then groaned. "Five-fifteen in the morning. Why so early?"

"Couldn't sleep."

"So you thought you'd just march in here and make sure I didn't get a full eight hours."

"As if you need that much."

The way he remembered, she seldom got more than five hours. He often woke up to find her in the middle of some project or another. Emily was one of those people who bounced out of bed and was fully functional before she brushed her teeth.

"It's going to be a long day." She drank her coffee and dramatically rolled her eyes. "Plane rides can be so very exhausting."

"Here's the deal," he said. "There aren't any direct flights from Aspen to San Francisco. You'll be routed through Denver first."

Watching him over the rim of her mug, she nodded agreement.

"Since we're already there, let's make a scheduled stop in Denver, spend the night and talk to Dylan. We'll still be investigating. Didn't you say you were looking for documents about imports and exports? He could hack in to Wynter Corp."

"Information obtained through illegal hacking can't be used for evidence."

"But you're not a cop," he said. "You don't have to follow legal protocols."

"True, and a hack could point me in the right direction. Dylan could also check company memos mentioning the murder victim. And, oh my God, accounting records." She came to an abrupt halt, set down her coffee and stared at him. "Why are you making this offer?"

"I want to help you with your new career."

Though he truly wished her well, helping her investigation wasn't the primary reason he'd suggested a stop in Denver. Sean wanted to derail her trip to San Francisco and keep her out of danger. As far as he was concerned, the world had enough investigative journalists. But there was only one Emily Peterson.

Her gaze narrowed. "Are you lying?"

He scoffed. "Why would I lie?"

"Turning my question into a different question isn't an answer." A slow smile lifted one corner of her mouth. "It's a technique that liars use."

"Believe whatever you want." He rose from her bed and placed his half-empty coffee mug on the bedside table. "I'm suggesting that you use Dylan because he's skilled, he has high-level contacts and he won't get caught."

She threw off the covers and went up on her knees. An overlarge plaid flannel top fell from her shoulders and hung all the way to her knees. The shirt looked familiar. He reached over and stroked the sleeve that she'd rolled up to the elbow. "Is this mine?"

"The top?" Unlike him, she was a terrible liar. "Why would I wear your jammies?"

"Supersoft flannel, gray Stewart plaid from L.L.Bean," he said. "I'm glad you kept it."

"I hardly ever wear flannel. But I was coming to Colorado and figured I might want something warm." She tossed her head, flipping her hair. "I forgot this belonged to you."

Another lie. He wondered if she'd been thinking of him when she packed her suitcase for this trip. Did she miss him? When she wore his clothing to bed, did she imagine his embrace?

He stepped up close to the bed and glided his arms around her, feeling the softness of the flannel plaid and her natural, sweet warmth. She'd been cozy in bed, wrapped in his pajamas that were way too big for her.

She cleared her throat. "What are you doing?"

"I'm holding you so you won't get cold."

He stroked her back, following the curve of her spine and the flare of her hips. With his hands still on the outside of the fabric, he cupped her full, round ass. Her body was incredible. She hadn't changed in the years they'd been apart. If anything, she was better, more firm and toned. He lifted her toward him, and she collapsed against his chest, gasping as though she'd been holding her breath.

"Ground rules," she choked out. "This is where we really need rules."

He lifted her chin, gazed into her face and waited until she opened her eyes. "You're supposed to be the spontaneous one, Emily. Let yourself go—follow your desires."

"I can't."

The note of desperation in her voice held him back. Though he longed to peel off the flannel top and drag her under the covers, he didn't want to hurt her. If she wanted a more controlled approach, he would comply.

"One kiss," he said, "on the mouth."

"Only one."

"And another on the neck, and another on your breast, and one more on…"

"Forget it! I should know better than to negotiate with you. There will be no kissing." She wriggled to get away from his grasp, but he wasn't letting go. "No touching. No hugging. No physical intimacy at all."

"You promised one," he reminded her.

"Fine."

She squinted her eyes closed and turned her face up to his. Her lips were stiff. And she was probably gritting her teeth. He'd still take the kiss. He knew what was behind her barriers. She still had feelings for him.

His kiss was slow and tender, almost chaste, until he began to nibble and suck on the fullness of her lower lip. His fingers unbuttoned the pajama top, and his hand slid inside. He traced a winding path across her torso with his fingertips, and when he reached the underside of her breast, she moaned.

"Oh, Sean." A shudder went through her. "I can't."

His hand stilled, but his mouth took full advantage of her parted lips. His tongue plunged into the hot, slick interior of her mouth.

She spoke again. "Don't stop."

She kissed him back. Her hand guided his to her nipples, inviting him to fondle. Her longing was fierce, unstoppable. Her body pressed hard against his.

And then it was over. She fell backward on the bed and buried herself, even her face, under the covers. He loved the way he affected her. As for the way she affected him? He couldn't ignore his palpitating heart and his rock-hard erection. But his attraction was more than that.

"About these ground rules," he said. "Don't tell me there's no physical intimacy allowed. If

I'm going to be around you and not allowed to touch, I'll explode."

"You scare me," she said as she crawled out from under the covers. "I don't want to fall in love with you again."

Would it really be so bad? She kept talking about how she had changed, but he was different, too. Not the same undercover agent that he was five years ago, he had learned tolerance, patience and respect.

Much of this shift in attitude came from his developing relationship with his brother; he was learning how to be a team player. Sean still teased—that was a big brother's prerogative—but he also could brush the small irritations away. At TST Security, he didn't insist on being the lead with every single job. He'd be nuts to interfere with Dylan's computer expertise, and their other partner, Mason Steele, was good at stepping in and taking charge.

His relationship with Emily was different. When they had been married, he might have been impatient. The way she kept prodding him about his work had been truly annoying. Why hadn't she been able to understand that undercover work meant he had to be secretive? If he kissed another woman while he was undercover, it didn't mean anything. How could it? In his mind, she was the perfect lover.

"First ground rule." He had to lay out parameters that allowed them to be together without hurting each other. "No falling in love."

"That's a good one," she said. "Write it down."

He sat at the small desk, found a sheet of notebook paper and a pen to jot down the first rule. "What about touching, kissing, licking, nibbling, sucking…" His voice trailed off as he visualized these activities. "I can't even say the words without needing to do it."

"I feel it, too, you know. We've always been amazing in bed, sexually compatible."

"Always."

In unison, they exhaled a regretful sigh.

"How about this?" she said. "No PDA."

Public display of affection? He wrote it down. "I can live with that."

She sat up on the bed and reached for her coffee mug again. After a sip, she proposed, "No physical contact unless I'm the one who initiates it."

He didn't like the way that sounded. "I need to have some kind of voice."

"You mean talking dirty?"

"Not necessarily. I might say something like I want to touch your cheek." Illustrating, he glided his hand along the line of her jaw, and then he leaned closer. "I want to kiss your forehead."

When he kissed her lightly, she pushed his

face away. "You can ask, but I have veto power. At any time, I can say no."

"So you have veto power and you can also initiate."

"Yes."

"What does that leave for me?" he asked as he returned to sit at the desk.

She cast him an evil smile. "Begging?"

"I'm not writing that down."

As far as he was concerned, their negotiation was taking a negative turn. The way she described it, she controlled all physical contact. She had all the power. No way would he be reduced to begging. There had to be another way to work it out.

As he doodled with the pen on the paper, he heard the ringtone from the cell phone in his pocket. "Finally we have communication from the outside world."

"Who is it?"

"The caller ID says Zebra929. So it has to be my brother. Dylan likes to play with the codes."

As soon as he answered, his brother said, "This is a secured call, bouncing the signal. It needs to be short."

"Shoot."

"I got a call from FBI Special Agent Levine out of San Francisco. Guess who he's trying to contact?"

"Emily Peterson," Sean said. A chill slithered down his spine. This was bad news.

"Whoa, are you psychic?"

"I'm looking right at her."

"Emily Peterson Timmons?"

Sean heard the amazement in his brother's tone.

"Emily the poet? Emily with the long hair? Your ex-wife?"

"What was the message from Levine?"

"He wanted to warn her. There's a leak in SFPD. Wynter might know her identity."

"Why did Levine call me?"

"He's grasping at straws," Dylan said. "None of her San Francisco contacts know where she went."

"What about her parents?"

"I asked the same question. The Petersons are out of the country."

Actually, that was good news. A threat to Emily could mean other people in her family might become targets for Wynter. Sean asked, "Did Levine mention an aunt in the mountains? A woman named Hazel?"

"Is that the Hazel Hopkins you took a contract with?"

Sean's pulse quickened. Not only had he received phone calls from Hazel, but he'd looked her up on the internet. It had taken nothing but a phone call for Levine to track him down. If

Frankie Wynter figured out that connection, he might hack in to TST Security phones or computers. They could find Hazel. "How secure are our computers?"

"Very safe," Dylan said. "But anything can be hacked."

"Wipe any history concerning Hazel Hopkins."

"Okay. We should wrap up this call."

"Thanks, Zebra. I'll be flying back to Denver today with Emily. We need your skills."

He ended the call and looked toward her. No more fun and games. She was in serious danger.

Chapter Six

Emily watched Sean transformed from a sexy ex to the hard-core FBI agent she remembered from their marriage. His devilish grin became tight-lipped. Twin worry lines appeared between his eyebrows. His posture stiffened.

She didn't like the direction his phone call was taking. As soon as he ended the call, she asked, "Why were you talking to your brother about Hazel?"

"If you're in danger, so is your family."

"Not Hazel. Our last names aren't the same. Nobody knows we're related."

"Can you be one hundred percent sure of that?"

"Not really."

When she'd first started writing articles that might be controversial, she disguised her identity behind a couple of pseudonyms. She didn't want to accidentally embarrass her mom and dad or her sister in law school, and she liked being a lone crusader. Anonymous and brave, she dug behind the headlines to expose corruption.

One of her best articles dealt with a cheating handyman who overcharged and didn't do the work. Another exposed a phone scam that entrapped the unwary. This story about Wynter Corp was her first attempt to investigate serious crime.

She should have known better. A personal threat was bad enough, but she'd brought danger to her family. Her spirits crumbled as she sat on the bed listening to Sean's recap of the phone call with his brother. This was her fault, all her fault.

Moments ago, she'd been kissing her gorgeous ex-husband and had been almost happy. Now she felt like weeping or hiding under the covers and never coming out. Why couldn't the blizzard have lasted forever? The snow would have hidden her.

Trying to soothe herself, she rubbed the soft fabric of her sleeve between her thumb and forefinger. Despite what she'd told him, she hadn't worn this top by accident; she knew very well that it belonged to Sean. Cuddling up in his pajamas always gave her a feeling of warmth and safety. Sometimes she closed her eyes and pretended that she could still smell his scent even though the pajamas had been laundered a hundred times.

He sat beside her and took her hand. "Are you okay?"

"Not at all." She heard the vulnerability in her voice and hated it. "You probably want to tell me that I never should have done this article, that I'm a girlie girl and should stick with poetry."

He squeezed her hand. "As I recall, your poetry wasn't all lollipops and sparkles. There was something about a fire giver and vultures that ate his liver."

"Prometheus," she remembered. "He started out trying to do the right thing, just like me. And then he was eternally damned by the gods. Is that my fate?"

"You made some mistakes, had some bad luck."

"I'm being a drama queen." She was well aware of that tendency and tried to tamp the over-the-top histrionics before she threw herself into full-on crazy mode. "Tell me I'm exaggerating."

"It's safe to say you're not really cursed by the gods," he said, "but don't underestimate the seriousness of this threat."

"I won't." Her lower lip trembled. She fought the tears that sloshed behind her eyelids. "Oh God, what should I do?"

"No crying." He held her chin and turned her

face so they were eye to eye. "You told me you were an investigative journalist. Well, you need to start acting like somebody who stands behind her words and takes responsibility for her actions."

His dark gaze caught and held her attention. His calm demeanor steadied her. Still, she was confused. "I don't know how."

"You're not Prometheus, and you're not little Miss Sunshine the poetry girl. Think of yourself as a reporter who got into trouble. What should we do next?"

"Make sure my family is safe."

Her parents were currently out of the country, visiting friends in the South of France. She didn't need to worry about Mom and Dad. Her three sisters were back east, and the two who were still in school lived alone. It seemed unlikely that Wynter would hunt them down. Nonetheless, they should be warned. "I should call my sisters."

"I'm going to ask you to wait until we get to Denver," he said. "The signal from your phone might be traced, and Dylan has equipment that's extremely secure."

"What about you?" She pointed to his cell phone. "What about that call?"

"It originated from the TST Security offices behind strong, thick firewalls."

She sat beside him, struggling to think in spite of the static waves that sizzled and shivered inside her head. From outside her bedroom door, she heard her aunt chattering to Willis as they went downstairs. It was early, a little after six o'clock and not yet dawn, but they were both already awake. Did they sleep together last night? Emily smiled to herself. *Ironic!* The senior citizens were getting it on while she and Sean stayed in separate bedrooms.

"I need to talk to Hazel." She looked toward him for guidance. "How much should I tell her?"

"She already knows you've witnessed a murder, so it won't come as a big shock that she's in danger. Until this is over, I'd advise her to leave Hazelwood, maybe stay in a hotel in Aspen."

"I'm guessing that Willis might have an extra bedroom," she said. "And he would probably be a good protector."

"A former deputy," Sean said. "I'd trust him."

And she didn't think it would take much to convince Hazel to spend more time with Willis. Emily's eccentric aunt had never remarried after her husband had died fifteen years ago, but she had taken several live-in lovers. Willis had always been a friend. Maybe it was time for him to be something more.

She picked up her coffee mug from the bedside table and drained it in a few gulps. Today was going to be intense, and she'd need all the energy she could muster. "After taking care of the family, what do I do?"

"It's up to you."

"The first thing that comes to mind is run and hide." That was exactly what the old Emily would have done. She would have hidden behind her big, strong husband. But that wasn't her style, not anymore. "I want to take responsibility. I'll go after the story."

He shrugged. "San Francisco, here we come."

With Sean at her side, she could handle the threat. She could take down James Wynter and his son. What she couldn't do was…forget. The blood spreading across Roger Patrone's white shirt flashed in her mind. The sounds of a beating and fading cries for help echoed in her ears. She could never erase the memory of murder.

OVER COFFEE IN the kitchen, Emily convinced Hazel that there was a real potential for danger and she ought to move in with Willis. It didn't take much persuasion. Hazel agreed almost immediately, and she was happy, as perky as a chipmunk. Her energy and the afterglow of excitement confirmed Emily's suspicion that her aunt and Willis were more than friends.

Hazel dashed upstairs to her bedroom to pack a few essentials, and Willis swaggered around the kitchen, talking to Sean about how he should make sure Hazel was safe and secure. Though Emily had a hard time imagining Willis the kind-hearted former deputy facing off with Wynter's thugs, she believed he was competent. Plus, he had the advantage of experience. He knew how to handle the dangers of the mountains and to use the elements to his advantage. His plan was to take Hazel to a ski hut he'd built on the other side of Aspen. The hut was accessible only by snowmobile or cross-country skis.

"What about the blizzard?" she asked.

Willis squinted out the kitchen window at a brilliant splash of sunlight reflecting off a pristine snowbank. "The big storm gave up during the night. We only got twenty or so inches, probably not even enough to close down the airport in Aspen."

She'd lived in San Francisco for so long that she'd forgotten how dramatically Colorado weather could change. Yesterday was a blizzard. Today she could get sunburned from taking a walk outside.

The timer on the oven buzzed. Emily opened the door, and the scent of sweet baked goods rushed toward her. Hazel had popped in a frozen almond-flavored coffee cake to thaw. Not as good as fresh made but decent enough for a rushed breakfast.

Willis went upstairs to help Hazel, and Emily turned toward Sean. "We need plane reservations to Denver," she said. "I'll go ahead and make them."

"You shouldn't." He pointed out the obvious.

"Just in case the bad guys have a way to track airline tickets, you ought to avoid using your real name."

"No problem." Her solution was sort of embarrassing, and she really didn't want to tell him. She placed the pan of coffee cake on a trivet on the counter and cut off a slab. With this breakfast in hand, she headed toward the exit from the kitchen. "I'm going to get packed, and then I'll call the airlines."

He blocked the exit. "I hope you aren't thinking about buying plane tickets with a fake ID and credit card. That kind of ploy can get you on the no-fly list."

"It's not exactly fake," she muttered. "Just out of date by about five and a half years."

As realization dawned, his eyes darkened. "The way I remember, you changed your name back to Peterson after the divorce."

"I did."

"Please don't tell me you're using your married name."

"The identity was just sitting there. I doctored an old driver's license and applied for a credit card as Emily Timmons, using my own Social Security number and my address in San Francisco. It works just fine."

"The no-fly list and fraud." Still blocking her way so she couldn't run, he glared at her. A muscle in his jaw twitched. "Anything else you want to tell me?"

"If I confess everything, we'll have nothing to discuss on the flight." She patted his cheek and slipped around him. "You can make the reservations."

"For today, you'll be Mrs. Timmons. And then no more."

"Don't count on it."

"What's that supposed to mean? Are you planning some kind of strange reconciliation that I don't know about?"

"This has nothing to do with you," she said coolly. "But I might need your name for fake identification."

With her almond cake in one hand and coffee in the other, she climbed the staircase and went to her bedroom. She sat at the small desk and activated one of her disposable phones. She couldn't wait until they got to Denver to contact her sisters. If Sean didn't like it, too bad. She really didn't think Wynter would go after them, but they deserved a heads-up. Michelle, who was in law school, asked how she could get in touch with Emily if she heard anything.

"You can't call me back."

"I know," Michelle said. "The phone you're using right now doesn't show up on my caller ID listing."

"Contact me through TST Security in Denver. I hired a bodyguard." Emily hoped to avoid mentioning her ex-husband. "They can get me a message."

"TST Security," Michelle repeated. "I'm looking them up on the internet right now. Found the website. Well, damn it, sis, here's an interesting coincidence. One of the owners of the aforementioned security firm happens to be Sean Timmons."

"I didn't call him."

"Really?" Michelle's tone dripped with sarcasm. "Do you want me to believe that he magically appeared when you were in trouble? Was he wearing a suit of armor and riding a white steed?"

"Aunt Hazel called him." Emily wanted to keep this conversation short. "And I don't have to justify my decisions to you or anybody else in the family."

"But justice will be served," said the future lawyer. "To tell the truth, Emily, I always liked Sean. I'm glad he's watching over you."

Emily avoided mentioning Sean to her other two sisters. Those calls ended quickly, and she jumped in the shower. Though she had time to wash and blow-dry her hair, she decided against it. Going out in the snow meant she'd be wearing a hat and squashing any cute styling.

She lathered up while her mind filled with speculation. No doubt, Michelle would blab to the rest of the family. And the questions would begin. *Would she get back together with him?* That seemed to be the query of the day. A few moments ago, Sean had asked about reconciliation.

Never going to happen. And her sisters should understand. Didn't they remember how devastated she'd been when she'd filed for divorce?

Their attitude about Sean had always been odd. When she first married him, the three sisters talked about how he was too old for her and his job was too dangerous for a stable relationship. In the divorce, however, the sister witches took Sean's side. They blamed her for being fickle and undependable when she should have been supportive. They told her to grow up. She couldn't always have things her own way.

Maybe true. Maybe she hadn't been the most understanding wife in the world. But he brought his own problems to the table: Being inflexible. Not taking her seriously. Concentrating too much on his work and not enough on his wife.

Wrapped in a towel after her shower, she padded into the bedroom and pulled out her luggage from under the bed. Since they were headed back to San Francisco, where she had clothes and toiletries at her apartment, she packed light. She tucked her three disposable cell phones in her carry-on. All data had already been downloaded off her de-activated computer.

She hid the flash drive in a specially designed black-and-silver pendant, which she wore on a heavy silver chain. A black cashmere sweater and designer jeans completed her outfit. Her practical boots and her parka were in the downstairs closet.

Before she left the bedroom, she checked her reflection in the mirror. *Not bad.* She didn't look as frazzled as she felt. Her hair was combed. Her lipstick properly applied. Her cheeks were flushed with nervous heat, but the high color might be attributed to too much blush.

Returning to San Francisco was the right thing to do, but she was sorely tempted to take off for a quickie Bahamas vacation with Sean. He owed her a trip. On their Paris honeymoon, he had held her hand in a sidewalk café and promised that every anniversary he would take her somewhere exciting. Their first anniversary rolled around and no trip. They couldn't get their schedules coordinated. And they argued about where to go. And when she told him to just forget it, he did.

What a brat she'd been! But at the time, she was too furious to make sense. She'd counted on Sean to be rational. That was his job. Somehow he should have known that even though she told him to forget it, he was supposed to lavish her with kisses and gifts until she changed her mind.

Their marriage had crumbled under the weight of hundreds of similar misunderstandings. Underneath it all, she wondered if they might actually be compatible. Certainly, there was nothing wrong with their sexual rapport. But could they talk? Was he too conservative? Were their worldviews similar? Was there any way, after the divorce, that she'd be willing to put her heart on the line and trust him? *I guess I'll find out.* While he was being her bodyguard and they were forced to be together, she had a second chance.

Chapter Seven

Clearing the runway in Aspen took longer than expected, and their flight as Mr. and Mrs. Timmons didn't land at DIA until after four o'clock in the afternoon. Sean rented a car and drove toward the TST office, where Dylan had promised to meet them.

In the passenger seat, Emily shed her parka and changed from snow boots to a pair of ballet flats. She peeked out the window at the undeveloped fields near the airport. "It's crazy. The snow's already melted."

"Denver only got a couple of inches."

"And the sky is blue, and the sun is shining. Every time I come back to Colorado, I wonder why I ever left."

"You don't have family in Denver, anymore."

"Nope." She gave him a warm smile. "But you do. I'm looking forward to seeing Dylan."

When Emily was being cordial, there was no

one more charming. Her voice was as sweet as the sound of a meadowlark. Her intense blue-green eyes sparkled. Every movement she made was sheer grace. It was hard to keep his hands off her.

Sitting close beside her on the plane, inhaling her scent and watching her in glimpses, had affected him. He was going to need more than a flimsy set of relationship "ground rules" to maintain control.

Following the road signs, he merged onto I-70. His real problem would come tonight. Their flight to San Francisco was scheduled for tomorrow morning at about ten o'clock, which meant they'd be sleeping in the same place tonight. After the stop at TST, he intended to take her to his home, where the security was high and he could keep an eye on her. He had an extra bedroom. What he didn't have was willpower. When she was in bed, just down the hall, he would be tempted.

"Sean?"

He realized that she'd been talking while he wasn't listening. "Sorry, what did you say?"

"How did you name your company? I get that TST stands for your initials, Timmons, Timmons and your other partner, Mason Steele. But your logo is a four-leaf clover with three green leaves and one a faded red."

"At one time, there were four of us." Sean

had told this story dozens of times, but his chest still tightened. Some scars never heal. This deep sadness would never go away. "We grew up together. Me and Dylan lived down the block from Mason and Matt Steele. Matt was my best friend. We were close in age, went to the same school, played on the same teams and went on double dates. When we were kids we pretended to be crime fighters."

"And when you grew up, you decided to fight crime for real."

"Not at first," he said. "We went to different colleges, followed our own separate ways. Matt joined the marines, and he liked the military life. That was why he couldn't be our best man. He was deployed, working his way up the chain of command."

There must have been a hint of doom in his tone, because Emily went very still. She listened intently.

He cleared his throat and continued. "About five years ago, Matt was killed in Afghanistan. His heroic actions rescued three other platoons, and he received a posthumous Purple Heart."

"I'm so sorry," she whispered.

"His death came right about the time our divorce was final. And I'd finished a sleazy undercover job where a good lawyer got the bad guys off with a slap on the wrist."

Remembering those dark days left a sour taste

in his mouth. He'd just about given up. Life was a joke, not worth living. He went on an all-out binge, drugs and alcohol. Thanks to his under-cover work, he was familiar with the filthy underbelly of the city, and he went there. He found rock bottom while seeking poisonous thrills that could wipe away his sorrow and regret and the senseless guilt that he was still alive while his friend was not. His judgment was off. He took stupid risks, landing in the hospital more than once. His path was leading straight to hell.

She reached across the console and touched his arm. "If I had known…"

"There was nothing you—or anybody else—could do. I didn't ask for help, didn't want anybody holding my hand."

"How did you get better?"

"I came back to Colorado and got on a physical schedule of weight lifting and running ten miles a day. I visited places where Matt and I used to go." He paused. "This sounds cheesy, but I found peace. I quit mourning Matt's death and celebrated his life."

"Not cheesy at all," she said.

"Weak?"

"That's the last word I'd use to describe you."

"Anyway, I did a lot of wilderness camping. One morning, I crawled out of my tent, stared up into a clear blue sky and decided I wanted a future."

"TST Security?"

"I quit the FBI, contacted my two buds and set up the business. I'd like to think that Matt would approve. We don't take cases that we don't like. And there are times like now when we can actually do some good."

"Is that how you think of my investigation into Wynter Corp?" She brightened. "As something that could make a difference?"

"I guess I do feel that way."

He hadn't realized until this moment that he wanted Frankie Wynter to pay the price for murder. Plus, they might take down members of a powerful crime family, and that felt good.

Exiting the interstate, they were close enough to downtown Denver for him to point out changes in the city where she'd lived for so many years. Giant cranes loomed over new skyscrapers—tall office buildings and hotels to accommodate the tourists. New apartment buildings and condos had popped up on street corners, filling in spaces that seemed too small. Denver was thriving.

Sean applauded the growth. More people meant more business and more opportunity. But he missed the odd, eclectic neighborhoods that were being swallowed by gentrification. Like most Denver natives, he was stubbornly protective of his city.

He parked the rental car in a small six-car lot

behind a three-story brick mansion near downtown. "We're here."

"Your office is in a renovated mansion." She beamed. "I can't believe you chose such a unique place."

"It's not unusual. This entire block is mansions that have been redone for businesses. We have the right half of the first floor. On the left side, there are three little offices—a life coach, a web designer and a woman who reads horoscopes. We all share the kitchen and the conference rooms upstairs."

"About the horoscope lady, what kind of conference meetings does she have?"

"Séances."

He opened the back door for her and held it while she entered an enclosed porch that was attached to the very modern kitchen with stainless steel appliances and a double-door refrigerator. It smelled like somebody had just microwaved a bag of popcorn.

"I love it," Emily said. "When you worked for the FBI, you never would have gone for a place like this."

"I've changed."

They went down the hallway to the spacious foyer with a grand staircase of carved oak and high ceilings. To the right, he stopped beside a door with an opaque glass window decorated with old-fashioned lettering for TST Security and their four-leaf clover logo. Using a keypad, Sean plugged in a code to open the door. Before he followed Emily inside, he touched the red leaf that represented Matt, as he always did.

Dylan greeted his former sister-in-law with enthusiasm, throwing his long arms around her for a big hug. He and Sean were the same height, but Dylan seemed taller because he was skinny. During his early years, Dylan was the epitome of a ninety-eight-pound weakling with oversize glasses and a permanent slouch. Sean had taken his little brother under his wing and got him working out. Under his baggy jeans and plaid flannel shirt, Dylan was ripped now.

They had two desks in the huge front office, but that wasn't where Dylan wanted to sit. He dragged her over to a brown leather sofa. On the coffee table in front of the sofa were snacks: popcorn, crackers and bottles of water.

She reached up to tuck a hank of brownish-blond hair behind his ear. "Almost as long as mine. I like the ponytail."

"I remember your super-long hair," he said.

"It was always such a mess."

"Not to me. It was beautiful. But I like this new look."

"Sorry to interrupt," Sean said, "but whenever you're done comparing stylists, there are some very bad men after Emily, and we need to take them out of the picture."

"Impatient," Dylan said as he pushed his horn-rimmed glasses up on his nose. He turned to Emily. "There's no need to be nervous in the TST office. It's one of the most secure spots in Denver. We've got bulletproof glass in the windows, sensors, surveillance cameras all around and sound-disabling technology so nobody can electronically eavesdrop."

"That's very reassuring." She opened a bottle of water and took a sip. "Can you make my computer un-hackable?"

"I can make it real hard to get in." Dylan pushed his glasses up again. "I've got an update."

"Another call from Agent Levine?" Sean guessed as he sat on the opposite end of the sofa from Emily.

"Levine isn't comment-worthy." Dylan plunked himself into a high-back swivel chair on wheels and paddled from a desk to the sofa. "I'm not insulting you, but the feds aren't real efficient."

"No offense taken," Sean said.

"This call was a few hours ago, a man's voice. He claimed to be an old friend from San Francisco. He identified himself as Jack Baxter. Sound familiar?"

"Not a bit," Sean responded. "Emily, do you know the name?"

"I don't think so."

Sitting on the big leather sofa with her hands

in her lap and her ankles crossed, she looked nervous and somewhat overwhelmed. Dylan could be a lot to take; he tended to bounce around like an overeager puppy.

Also, Sean reminded himself, she was aware of the threat, the potential for danger. He directed his brother. "We need to focus here. What did Baxter want?"

"Supposedly, he was just thinking of you, his old pal. It seemed too coincidental for you to be contacted by a supposed friend on the same day Levine called." He shot a look at Emily. "He kept asking about you. Suspicious, right?"

Sean remained focused. "Did you track the call?"

"He claimed to be in San Francisco, and his cell phone had the 414 area code. But I triangulated the microwave signal." Dylan paused for effect. "He was calling from DIA."

Emily shot to her feet. "He's here? At the Denver airport?"

Dylan winced. "It gets worse. I ran a reverse lookup on the cell phone. It belongs to John Morelli."

"I know him," she said. "He works for Wynter."

"Bingo," Dylan said. "I've been doing a bit of preliminary hacking on Wynter. And Morelli is vice president in charge of communication."

"That's right," Emily said. "I interviewed him

for my first article on Wynter Corp. He's the only person I spoke to in person."

"Which might be why he was sent to Denver to find you," Sean said. "When you met with him, did you use the Timmons alias?"

She shook her head. "Timmons is only for travel and the one credit card. I use another alias for my articles and interviews."

"How did Wynter make the connection between us?"

Dylan rolled toward him on the swivel chair. "Remember how I said the feds were idiots? Well, I think Wynter had their phones tapped. When Levine called here, looking for you, I told him you weren't involved with Emily. But the contact must have sent up a red flag to Wynter."

His deduction made sense. "I want you to dig deeper into Wynter Corp. Check into their bank accounts and expenses."

"Forensic accounting." Dylan nodded. "Will do."

"How much can you find out?" Emily asked. "That information belongs to Wynter Corp. It's protected."

"I've got skills," Dylan said, "and I can hack practically anything. Unlike the feds, I don't have to worry about obtaining the evidence through illegal means because I don't plan to use the data in court. This is purely a fact-finding mission."

She accepted him at his word. "Concentrate

on the import-export business. Check inventories against shipping manifests—look for warehouse information."

"I took a peek earlier," Dylan said. "They also handle real estate, restaurants and small businesses."

"For now I'm looking for evidence of smuggling and human trafficking." She bounced to her feet. "I have information that will give you a starting point."

"Cool," Dylan said. "If you give me the flash drive you've got hidden in your necklace, I'll get started."

"How did you know?" She touched her black-and-silver pendant. "Is it obvious?"

"Only to me," he said as he held out his flat palm.

Although Sean didn't speak up and steal his brother's thunder, he had also figured out where she was hiding her flash drive. *Simple logic.* All day long, she'd been touching her pendant, guarding it. What would she want to protect? Her most precious possession was her work; therefore, he guessed she had her documents on a flash drive. And she'd hidden it in chunky jewelry that wasn't her usual style.

Dylan rolled his chair to a computer station with four display screens and three keyboards. Emily followed behind him, eager to learn the magic techniques that allowed Sean's brother to dance across the World Wide Web like a spider with a ponytail and horn-rimmed glasses.

Long ago Sean had given up trying to understand how Dylan did what he did. The technical aspects of security and investigative work had never interested Sean. He learned more from observing, questioning the people involved and creating a profile of the criminals and the victims. When he'd gone undercover for the FBI, he had to rely on instinct to separate the good guys from the bad. And his gut was good. He was seldom wrong.

He left the sofa and sauntered across the large, open room with high ceilings to the window. It bothered him that John Morelli was in Denver. Dylan's theory of how Wynter got his name had the ring of truth. Tapping the FBI phones was depressingly obvious.

His brother and Emily stared at the screens as though answers would materialize before their eyes. Sean hardly remembered a time when computers weren't a part of life, but he'd never fallen in love with the technology and he hated the way people stumbled around staring at their cell phones. His brother called him a Luddite, and maybe he was. Or maybe he'd made the decision, when they were kids, that computers would be Dylan's thing. Whatever the case, it appeared that Dylan and Emily would be occupied for a while.

Sean announced, "I'm going out to pick up some dinner. Is Chinese okay?"

Barely looking away from the screens, they both murmured agreement.

"Any special requests?"

The response was another mumble.

He went to a file cabinet near the door, unlocked it and took out a Glock 17. He had to pack both of his handguns on the plane and take out the bullets. For the moment, it was quicker to grab the semiautomatic pistol and insert a fresh magazine into the grip. He was almost out the door when Emily ran up behind him and grasped his arm.

"You shouldn't go out there," she said. "Mr. Morelli could be waiting in ambush."

"Mr.?"

"That's what I called him in the interview. He's older, in his forties."

"If he was sneaking around, close enough to show up on Dylan's surveillance, we'd be hearing a buzzer alarm."

She kissed his cheek. "Be careful."

It had been a long time since anybody was worried about his safety. He kind of liked being fussed over.

At the back door, he paused to peer into the trees that bordered the parking lot. There were garages and Dumpsters in the alley behind their office, lots of hiding places if Morelli had staked out the office.

He went down the stairs and got into the rental car to pick up food from Happy Food Chinese restaurant. Then, he backed out into the alley. In less than a mile, he noticed a black sedan following him. Wynter's men had found him. And he'd made it easy. *Damn it, I should have ordered delivery.*

Chapter Eight

Emily watched the numbers unfurling across two screens while Dylan used a third screen to enter the forbidden area of the dark web where you could buy or sell anything. Pornographers, killers, perverts and all types of scum hung out on those mysterious, ugly sites.

She looked away. "What's a nice guy like you doing in a place like that?"

"If you want to get the dirt, you can't keep your hands clean."

Even though her investigation was for a worthy cause, she didn't like spying. Hacking broke one of the ethical rules of journalism that said you needed at least two sources for every statement before you could call it a fact. And they had to be credible sources. Some bloggers just fabricated their stories from lies and rumors. She wasn't like that. Not irresponsible. The thought jolted her. *Wow, have I changed!* When she was married to Sean, he'd complained about her lack of responsibility. Now she was saying the same about other people.

She strolled across the room to a window and looked out at the fading glow of sunset reflected on the marble lions outside the renovated mansion across the street. "We shouldn't have let Sean go without backup."

"He can take care of himself," Dylan said. "He took a gun."

And that worried her, too. If he wasn't expecting trouble, why did he make sure he was armed? "We should go after him."

"Call him." Dylan gestured to the old-fashioned-looking phone on the other desk. "Press the button for extension two. That rings through to his cell phone."

"Are you extension number one?"

"No way." He glanced over his shoulder at her. "That number is, and always will be, Mom."

"Sean told me that your parents are still in Denver."

"And my mother would lo-o-o-ve to see you and Sean get back together. Her dream is grand-babies."

"I heard you're dating someone."

"Her name is Jayne. It's a serious relationship." His eyes lit up. "But we aren't talking about babies."

From the sneaky smile on his face, she could

tell that the topic of marriage had come up. Little brother Dylan had found a woman who would put up with his computers. She was happy for him.

As she tapped the extension on the office phone, she hoped that she was worrying about nothing. Sean would pick up and tell her he was fine.

From the other side of the desk, she heard his ringtone. Then she saw his cell phone next to the computer screen. He hadn't taken the phone with him.

"Dylan, we have to go." She hung up the phone. "We have to help Sean."

He lifted his hands off the keys and looked up at her. "Is there something about this Morelli person that I don't know about? Is he particularly dangerous?"

Her impression of the man she'd interviewed was that he was a standard midlevel management guy. He'd worn a nice suit without a necktie. His shoes were polished loafers. His best feature was his thick black hair, which was slicked back with a heavy dose of styling gel. When he spoke he did a lot of hemming and hawing, and she had the sense that he wasn't telling her much more than she could learn from reading about Wynter Corp on the internet.

"Not dangerous," she said. "He was the contrary. Quiet, secretive. Morelli is the kind of guy who fades into the woodwork."

"I'm guessing my brother can handle him."

"I hate to say this." But she remembered those horrible moments on the boat when Patrone was killed. "What if Morelli's not alone?"

That possibility lit a fire under Dylan's tail. He was up and out of his computer chair in a few seconds. He motioned for her to follow, and she ran after him. They raced out the front door and onto the wide veranda to an SUV parked at the curb.

SEAN WOULD HAVE known right away that he was being followed if it hadn't been the middle of rush hour with the downtown streets clogged and lane changing nearly impossible. He first caught sight of a black sedan when he was only three blocks away from the office. After he doubled back twice, he was dead certain that the innocent-looking compact sedan, probably a rental from the airport, was on his tail.

Weaving through the other cars on Colfax Avenue, his pursuer had to stay close or risk losing Sean in the stop-and-go traffic. A couple of times, the sedan was directly behind Sean's car. At a stoplight, he studied the rearview mirror, trying to figure out if Morelli was by himself or with a partner.

He appeared to be alone.

Emily had described him as being in his forties. That was the only information Sean had. He should have asked for more details, but he didn't want to alarm her. Leaving the office without a plan had been an unnecessary risk. He knew that. So why had he done it? Was he feeling left out while Dylan did his thing with the computers? Jealous of his little brother?

Envy might account for 5 percent of his decision, but mostly he'd wanted time alone to refresh his mind. Ever since he saw Emily, he'd been tense. And when they kissed…

He checked his side mirror. The black sedan was one car back, still following. Dusk was rapidly approaching. Some vehicles had already turned on their headlights. If he was going to confront the man in the sedan, he should make his move. Darkness would limit his options.

Sean didn't necessarily want to hurt Morelli. He wanted to talk to the guy, to have him send a message back to James Wynter that Sean wasn't somebody to mess around with, and he was protecting Emily. The bad guys needed to realize that she wasn't helpless, and—in his role as her bodyguard—he wouldn't hesitate to kick ass.

He set a simple trap. Accelerating and making a few swerving turns, he sped into a large, mostly empty parking lot at the west end of Cherry Creek Mall. Sean fishtailed behind a building, parked and jumped out of the car before the black sedan came around the corner.

His original plan had been to hide behind his car, but a better possibility appeared. Though the parking lot was bare asphalt right now, there had been snow that morning. The plows had cleared the large lot and left the snow in a waist-high pile near a streetlight. Sean dove behind it.

Holding his gun ready, he watched and waited while the black sedan cautiously inched closer and closer. It circled his car, keeping a distance. The sedan parked behind his car, and a man got out. He braced a semiautomatic pistol with both hands.

"Sean Timmons," he shouted. "Get out of the car. I'm not going to hurt you."

"You got that right." Sean came out from behind the snow barrier. His position was excellent, in back of the driver of the sedan. "Drop the gun and raise your arms."

If it came to a shoot-out, he wouldn't hesitate to drop this guy. But he wouldn't take the first shot. The man set his gun on the asphalt, raised his hands and turned. "We need to talk."

Since they were standing in view of a busy street with rush hour traffic streaming past, Sean lowered his gun as he approached the other man. In spite of the gun, this guy didn't seem real threatening. Dressed in a conservative blue sweater with khaki trousers, he wore his hair slicked back. His pale complexion hinted that he spent most of his time indoors.

Sean asked, "Is your name Morelli?"

"John Morelli."

"Are you a hit man, John?"

"Of course not."

"What do you want to say?"

"It's about your ex-wife." He took a step forward and Sean raised his gun, keeping him back. "If you'll let me talk to her, I can explain everything."

He sounded rational, but Sean wasn't convinced. "You could have called her," he pointed out.

"I tried," Morelli said. "I left messages on her answering machine. She's a hard woman to reach, especially since she gave me a fake name."

That much was true. "How did you find out her real name?"

Morelli didn't answer immediately. He exhibited the classic signs of nerves: furrowed brow, the flicker of an eyelid, the thinning of the lips and the clearing of his throat. All these tics and twitches were extremely subtle. Most people wouldn't notice.

But Sean was a pro when it came to questioning scumbags. He knew that whatever Morelli said next was bound to be a lie.

"It's like this," Morelli said. "I saw her on the street and followed her to her house."

"You stalked her?"

Quickly Morelli said, "No, no, it wasn't creepy. I guessed her neighborhood from something she said at our interview."

"Not buying that story."

"Okay, you got me." He tried a self-deprecating gesture that didn't quite work. "I got her fingerprint at our interview and ran it through identification software."

Sean had enough. "Here's what I think. Your boss, James Wynter, used an illegal wiretap, overheard her name. When he pulled up her photo, you recognized the reporter who interviewed you."

Morelli was breathing harder. A dull red color climbed his throat. "I don't know anything about illegal wiretaps, and I'm insulted that you think I would be that sort of person."

As if being a stalker was more reputable? "This is your last chance to be honest, Morelli. Otherwise, I'll turn you in to the feds. They keep an open file on Wynter, and they'll be interested in you."

"Wait!" He lowered his hands and waved them frantically. "There's no need for law enforcement."

"Don't tell me another lie."

"Truth, only truth, I swear."

Sean tested that promise by asking, "Did Wynter send you to Denver?"

"Yes."

"What were you supposed to do?"

"Find your ex-wife. When he said her name was Emily Peterson, I didn't know who he was talking about. I knew her as Sylvia Plath."

Sean stifled a chuckle. Emily's obviously phony alias referenced a famous poet. "What made you think she might come looking for me? Did you miss the 'ex' in front of husband?"

"After I learned that she'd gone on the run, I checked her background on the internet. Your name popped up, and I knew. The first person the girl would look to for help was her macho, ex-FBI husband who runs a security firm."

His story sounded legit. Or maybe Sean just enjoyed being called macho. He liked that he was the guy to call when danger struck. Or was he being conned?

Morelli was turning out to be a puzzle. He readily admitted that he worked for Wynter and he carried a gun, but he looked like a middle-aged man who had just finished a game of billiards in a sunless pool hall. He was less intimidating than a sock puppet.

Sean made a guess. "You don't get out of the office much, do you?"

"Not for a long time." He gave a self-deprecating smile. "I've had both knees replaced."

Scenes from old gangster movies where some poor shmuck was getting his kneecaps broken with a baseball bat flashed through Sean's mind. But he didn't go there. This was the twenty-first century, and criminals were more corporate... more like the man standing before him.

"There's something bothering me," Sean said. "When you called the TST office, you used your own phone."

"So? I wasn't giving anything away. My number's unlisted."

"An easy hack," Sean said. "I might even be able to do it."

"I should've used a burner." The corners of his mouth pulled down. He seemed honestly surprised and upset. *What is going on with this guy?* If Wynter hadn't sent him to wipe out the witness to his son's crime, why was Morelli here?

Sean said, "What were you supposed to do when you found my ex-wife?"

"To warn her."

"About what?"

"If she prints her article from information I gave her, it's going to have several errors. Wynter Corp is planning a significant move in regard to our real estate holdings."

As he spoke, his face showed signs that he was lying. His lip quivered. He even did the classic signal of looking up and to the right. For a thug, Morelli was a terrible liar.

"Seriously," Sean said. "You want me to believe that you rushed out to Denver, tailed my car through rush-hour traffic and pulled a gun so you could talk real estate?"

"Doesn't make sense, does it?"

"Last chance. Tell me the real reason. What do you want from Emily?"

"I want to find out what she knows."

His statement seemed sincere. "Why would you think Emily has information that you don't?"

"She's been researching Wynter Corp for quite a while, and it's possible she stumbled over some internal operations data that would be embarrassing to Mr. Wynter."

"Lose the corporate baloney. What's the problem?"

"Somebody's stealing from us, and we want to know who."

"Now you're talking." Sean believed him. Wynter wouldn't be happy about somebody dipping into his inventories. "Do you really think Emily might have information you missed? Is she that good an investigator?"

"Her first article on Wynter Corp was right on target."

It occurred to Sean that if he pretended that Emily had valuable information, the hit men wouldn't hurt her. Luckily, he was an excellent liar. "I shouldn't tell you, but she's come up with a working hypothesis. She's figured out what's happening on the inside. If she gets hurt, it all goes public."

"I knew it was an insider." Morelli cleared his throat. "And there's that other matter I need to discuss."

"The murder?"

"She might have imagined seeing something that did not, in fact, happen."

Sean shook his head. "She's sure of what she saw, and she won't be convinced otherwise."

"How much would it take to unconvince her?"

And now Sean had full comprehension. Morelli wasn't here to kill her. He'd come to Denver to seduce her into working for Wynter Corp with cash payoffs and assurances that she was brilliant. Clearly, he didn't know Emily.

It was time to wrap up this encounter. If Sean had still been a fed, he would've taken Morelli into custody and gone through a mountain of paperwork to come up with charges that would be dismissed as soon as Wynter's lawyers got involved. As a bodyguard, he didn't have those responsibilities. His job was to keep Emily safe.

He made a threat assessment. "Are there other Wynter operatives in Denver?"

"No."

But a quick twitch at the corner of his eye told Sean the opposite. "How many?"

For a moment, Morelli sputtered and prevaricated, trying to avoid the truth. Then he admitted, "One other person. He does things differently than I do."

Sean translated. "He's more of a 'shoot-first' type."

"You could say that."

He needed to get Emily out of town before the less subtle hit man caught up with them. He picked up Morelli's pistol, removed the ammo and returned it to him. At the same time, Morelli handed him a business card.

"It's got all my numbers," Morelli said.

"I'll get your message to Emily. If she agrees to talk to you, she'll call. Don't approach her or me again."

They walked away from each other, each returning to his separate rental car. As Sean slid behind the wheel, he wished that he could trust Morelli. It would've been handy to have an inside man at Wynter Corp.

As he drove to the homely, little Chinese restaurant where they always ordered carryout, he checked his rearview mirrors and scanned the traffic. There was no sign of Morelli. He didn't know what the other hit man—the more dangerous thug—would be driving.

At the restaurant, he spotted Dylan and Emily sitting at one of the small tables near the kitchen. He would have been annoyed that she'd left the security of the office and put herself in danger, but this happenstance worked for him.

She stood and faced him. "Next time," she said, "take your damn phone. I was worried."

"Ready to go?" he asked.

Dylan held up a large brown paper bag with streaky grease stains on the side. "It's our usual order."

"Bring it. I get hungry on plane rides."

Emily gaped. "Plane?"

Sean wasn't going to hang around in Denver, waiting for the second hit man to find them. For all he knew, Morelli had already contacted his partner-in-crime. Sean and Emily had to escape. The sooner, the better.

Chapter Nine

Emily had no idea how Sean accomplished so much in so little time. It seemed to be a combination of knowing the right people and calling in favors; she couldn't say for sure. Maybe he was magic. In any case, he'd told her that Denver was too dangerous, and within an hour she was on a private jet, ready to take off for San Francisco.

After she'd been whisked to a small airfield south of town, Sean rushed her into an open hangar and got her on board a Gulfstream G200. Her only other experience with private aircraft was a ski trip on a rickety little Cessna, which was no comparison to this posh eight-passenger jet. Sean left her with instructions not to disembark.

She strolled down the strip of russet-brown carpet that bisected the length of the cabin. Closest to the cockpit were four plush taupe leather chairs facing one another. Behind that was a long sofa below the porthole windows on one side

and two more chairs on the other. The galley—
a half-size refrigerator, cabinet, sink and microwave—was tucked into the rear.

Her stomach growled, and she made a quick
search of the kitchenette. There were three different kinds of water in the fridge and the liquor
cabinet was well stocked, but the cupboards were
almost bare.

At the front of the cabin, she sank into one of
the chairs. The cushioned seat and back cradled
her, elevating her to a level of comfort that was
practically a massage. Still, she didn't relax. A
persistent adrenaline rush stoked her nervous
energy.

Bouncing to her feet, she paced the length of
the aircraft, all the way to the bathroom behind
the galley to the closed door that separated the
cockpit from the cabin. Sean had left her suitcase, and she wondered if she should change out
of the black sweater she'd been wearing since before dawn this morning. A fresh outfit might give
her a new perspective, and she needed something
to lighten her spirits and ease her tension.

Not that she was complaining about the way
Sean had handled the threat from Morelli. He'd
done a good job, but she wished that she'd been
there. Somehow it felt like the situation was slipping through her fingers. She was losing control.

Or was she overreacting? The trip to San Francisco had originally been her idea, not his. But

she had new information and needed to reconsider. Sean should have consulted with her before charging into the breach and arranging for a private jet. She had opinions. This was her investigation. He wasn't the boss. When push came to shove, he was actually her employee.

A sense of dread rose inside her. She'd felt this way before. Frustrated and voiceless, she was reminded of the final, ugly days of their marriage. Until the bitter end, Sean had tried to make all the decisions. He wanted to be the captain who set their course while she was left to swab the decks and polish the hardware. Her only option had been mutiny.

In the past when she'd tried to stop him, she failed more than she succeeded. He was so implacable. And she didn't want to fight. *Make love, not war.* She'd changed. No longer a nineteen-year-old free spirit who tumbled whichever way the wind was blowing, the new Emily was solid, determined and responsible. As soon as she could get Sean alone, she meant to set the record straight.

Dylan stuck his head through the entry hatch. His long hair was out of the ponytail and hanging around his face, making him look like a teenager. "I brought you a brand-new, super-secure computer."

He sat and wiggled his butt. "Nice chair."

"Very." She sat opposite.

Obviously he'd been in this jet before. He knew exactly how to pull out a table from the wall. When it stretched out between them, he set a laptop on it, opened the lid and spun it toward her. "As I've said before, about a hundred times, anything can be hacked. This system has extreme firewalls, but when you're not using it, log off with this code."

He typed in numbers and letters that ran together: 14U24Me.

"One for you two for me," she read.

"Easy to remember." He reached into his backpack. "And here's your new cell phone, complete with camera and large screen. It's loaded with everything that was on your old phone, but this baby is also secure. It bounces your signal all around the world."

She stroked the smooth plastic cover. "I've missed having a phone."

"Yeah, well, don't get tempted to play with this. Keep texting to the bare minimum and don't add a bunch of apps. In the interest of security, keep your calls short. And when you aren't using the phone, log off."

"I thought cell phones could be tracked even when they were off."

"Not this one. Not unless somebody hacks my most recent software innovation, and that's not going to happen for a couple of weeks at least." Digging into his pocket, he produced her flash drive. "You can slip this back into your necklace. I've got a copy."

"While we're gone, will you keep hacking Wynter?"

"You bet."

"You might run comparisons between shipping manifests and inventory, plus sales figures."

He pushed the glasses up on his nose. "Morelli seemed convinced that there was theft. That gives me another angle."

In her research, she hadn't uncovered any evidence that someone was stealing from Wynter. But she hadn't been using the sophisticated hacking tools that Dylan so deftly employed. Part of her wanted to have him teach her; the more ethical part of her conscience held her back. Hacking wasn't a fair way to investigate.

Dylan stood. Before leaving, he gave her a brotherly kiss on the cheek. "I know Sean is supposed to be taking care of you. But keep an eye on him, okay? Don't let him do anything crazy dangerous."

"I'll try."

When Dylan left, she was alone in the cabin. Still seated, she peered through a porthole. Through the open door to her hangar, she could see one of the lighted runways, part of another hangar and several small planes tethered to the tarmac. The control tower was a four-story building with a 360-degree view that reminded her of some of the lighthouses up the coast in Oregon. As she watched, a midsize Cessna taxied to the far end of the airstrip, wheeled around and halted. With a burst of speed, the white jet sped forward and gracefully lifted off. Silhouetted against the night sky, the Cessna's lights soared to the right, toward the dark shadow of the mountains west of the city.

Sean came through the hatch and sat in the chair opposite her, where Dylan had been sitting. As easily as Dylan had pulled down the table, Sean removed that barrier between them. He leaned forward with his elbows resting on his knees.

"Are you okay?" he asked.

His gentleness threw her off guard. She noticed that he hadn't shaved, and dark stubble outlined his jaw. By asking how she was, he'd given her an opening to rationally discuss how she should be kept in the loop. Right now she should assert her needs and desires, let him know she was in charge. *Right now! This moment!*

Instead she stared dumbly at his face, distracted by the perfect symmetry of his features. Why did he have to be so gorgeous?

"Emily?" His eyebrows lifted as though her name were a question. "Emily, tell me."

"When did you find time to change?" He'd discarded his turtleneck for a cotton shirt and a light suede bomber jacket. She couldn't say he looked fresh as a daisy. Sean was much too rugged to be compared to a flower.

"Only took a minute," he said. "Are you—"

"You asked if I was okay." She stumbled over the words. "Okay about what?"

"Going to San Francisco," he said. "We're set to leave in ten minutes. A flight plan has been filed, but this is a private jet. You can change your mind and go anywhere."

She wasn't following. "What do you mean?"

"San Francisco is dangerous. There are alternative destinations, like Washington State or heading south to Mexico. We could even go to Hawaii."

Irritated, she pushed herself out of the cozy chair and stalked toward the rear. "I'm not afraid."

"I didn't say you were." He followed her down the aisle.

"But you think I might want to run away." She pivoted to face him. "Maybe I'd like to take a vacation in Hawaii and lie on the beach. Is that what you want? For me to hide in a safe place while Wynter runs his human trafficking ring and his son gets away with murder."

"It's not about what I want."

"I'm glad you understand." But she almost wished he'd be unreasonable. Making her point was easier when he argued against her. His rational approach meant she had to also be thoughtful.

"You don't have to step into the line of fire," he said. "You could keep researching the crimes on computer. Work with Dylan. There's no need for you to confront Wynter in his lair."

"I've considered that." There were threads of evidence that she needed to be in San Francisco to follow. With Sean to accompany her, she had more access.

"I need an answer on our destination."

"I've got a question for you," she said. "How do you rate a private jet?"

"Don't worry about it."

"I sincerely hope you're not charging my aunt some exorbitant fee."

"This trip is a favor, and it's free," he said. "You'll recognize the pilot from our wedding. David Henley."

She knew the name. "The guy who plays the banjo?"

"Flying planes is his real job."

"Good for him. He couldn't have made much of a living as a banjo picker."

"In addition to this sweet little Gulfstream, he has a Cessna, an old Sabreliner and two helicopters. He freelances for half a dozen or so companies, flying top execs around the country."

The aforementioned David Henley swung through the entry hatch and marched down the aisle toward them. "Emily, my princess. It's been a while."

Though David was an average-looking guy with wavy blond hair, she most certainly remembered him from the wedding. He'd hit on each of her sisters and ended up going home with her former roommate. He tapped Sean on the shoulder. "May I give this princess a hug?"

"Don't ask me," Sean said. "She can speak for herself."

He held his arms wide. "Hug?"

"Don't get too snuggly," she said. "I see that wedding band on your finger."

His arms wrapped around her. "I like to tease the princesses, but that's as far as it goes. My heart belongs to my queen, my wife."

"My former roommate." She remembered the announcement from a few years ago. "Please give Ginger a hug from me."

"She'll be bummed that she didn't have a chance to get together with you."

She preferred this mature version of David to the horny banjo player. "Thanks for the plane ride."

"I'm sorry you're in so much trouble." He held her by the shoulders and looked into her eyes. "Are we going to San Francisco?"

"Yes, so be sure to wear some flowers in your hair."

"Still cute." He turned toward Sean. "I won't be using you as copilot. This flight is a good opportunity to train the new guy I hired. Now, I've got to run some equipment checks before we take off. Ciao, you two."

While David went forward to the cockpit, she asked Sean, "You know how to fly a plane?"

"David's been teaching me. The helo is more fun." He gestured toward the seats across the aisle from the sofa bench. "Get comfortable. I'll see if he's got any food back here."

In the rush to get to the airfield, they'd forgotten the Chinese food. She couldn't honestly say she had regrets. Fast food from Denver didn't compare with San Francisco's Chinatown, but the remembered aroma tantalized her. Her stomach rumbled again. No doubt, Dylan would munch the chicken fried rice, chop suey, broccoli beef and General Tso's for dinner. With an effort, she managed to pull out the table between the two seats.

Sean didn't have much to put on it: Two small bags of chips and two sparkling waters. "This will have to do."

Not enough to appease her hunger, but it was probably good that she wouldn't be settling down and getting comfortable. Other than being starving, things seemed to be going her way. She wanted to go to San Francisco, and that was where they were headed. If she was smart, this would be a good time to stay quiet. But she wanted to lay down the basics of a plan for *her* investigation, with emphasis on *her*.

She cleared her throat. "I want to talk about what we're going to do when we land."

"Right," he agreed. "I need to make hotel reservations."

"We can stay in my apartment."

"You're joking."

"Not really."

He regarded her with a disbelieving gaze. "Morelli came all the way to Denver to find you. I'm guessing that Wynter's men have found your apartment."

"But they think I'm in Denver."

"These aren't the sort of guys to play cat and mouse with. As soon as they figure out where you really are, they'll be knocking at your door or busting a hole with a battering ram."

She deferred to his expertise. "Make the reservations."

"I like the Pendragon Hotel," he said. "It's near the trolley line and close to Chinatown."

"We're not going on a sightseeing trip."

The copilot boarded the jet, bringing cold cuts and bread for sandwiches. *Food!* She almost kissed him.

While she and Sean slapped together sandwiches, they dropped their discussion of anything important. The sight and smell of fresh-sliced ham and turkey and baby Swiss made her giddy. And the copilot hadn't stinted on condiments, providing an array of mustard, mayo, horseradish and extra-virgin olive oil. Her mouth was watering. Tomatoes, cucumbers, baby bib lettuce and coleslaw.

She sliced a tomato thin and placed it carefully on the ciabatta bread between the mustard and the lettuce. "I suppose we should make something for David and the copilot."

"We should." He glanced in her direction. "But you really don't look like you can wait for one more minute."

"I'm ravenous."

"Get started without me. I'll take food to the cockpit."

"Best offer I've had all day."

The sandwich she'd assembled was almost too big for her mouth, but she tore off a chunk and chomped down on it. The explosion of flavor in her mouth was total ecstasy. As the sandwich slid down her throat, she relished texture, the taste and the nourishment. She took another bite and another.

The last food she'd had was that morning in the mountains, and that felt like a lifetime ago. While she continued to eat, her eyelids closed. She groaned with pleasure.

After a few more bites, she opened her eyes to reach for her water and saw Sean standing behind his chair, looking down at her. He grinned and said, "Sounds like you're enjoying the sandwich. Either that or you've decided to join the Mile High Club all by yourself."

She swallowed a gulp of water. "How do you know I'm not already a member?"

"Are you?"

"No way," she said. "I'm pretty sure it takes two."

"I'd be happy to volunteer."

Standing there, he was devilish handsome with his wide shoulders, his tousled hair, his stubble and his hands, his rugged hands. Too easily, she imagined his gentle caress across her shoulders and down her back. His eyes, when they'd made love, turned the color of dark chocolate, and his gaze could make her melt inside.

She shoved those urges aside and returned her attention to the sandwich. She needed refueling. Before she was full, the Gulfstream taxied onto the runway.

"Don't bite my arm off," Sean said as he scooped up the remains of her sandwich. "The food has to move before takeoff. Or you'll be wearing it."

David opened the door from the cockpit. "Fasten your seat belts."

She buckled up, gripped the arms of her seat and braced herself as the whine of the engines accelerated and a tremor went through the jet. Though she'd actually never been afraid of flying or of heights, she suffered an instinctive twinge in her gut and a shimmer of vertigo when a plane took off or when she stood at the edge of a cliff. Again, she closed her eyes.

Her mind ran through various streams of evidence they'd investigate in San Francisco, ranging from a meeting with the feds to a possible reconnaissance on Wynter's luxury double-decker yacht.

In moments, they were airborne.

Her eyelids opened. She looked at Sean and said the first thing on her mind, "Don't let me forget Paco the Pimp."

"I'm hoping that's a nickname for something else."

"He's a real guy. I met him about a year ago when I was doing an article on preteen hookers." She shuddered. "That was a painful experience, one horrifying story after another. I almost decided to quit journalism and go back to soothing poetry or lyric writing. Paco changed my mind."

"By offering you a job?"

"Oh, he did that…several times. Not that either of us took his offers seriously. Anyway, he reminded me of my obligation to shine a light on the ugly truth in the hope that people would pay attention. And the horror would stop…or at least slow down."

He lowered himself into the seat opposite her and pulled out the table. Instead of returning the last few bites of her sandwich, he placed a bottle of red wine and two plastic glasses on the flat surface. "And why do you need to remember Paco?"

"He's got an ear to the street. He hears all the gossip. And I want to find out if he remembered anything from that night." She hesitated. Maybe she was bringing up a volatile topic. She didn't want Sean to be mad at her. "He might have seen something I missed."

He used a corkscrew to open the wine. "Are you talking about the night of the murder?"

Averting her gaze, she looked through the porthole window. The lights of Denver glittered below them. Ahead was the pitch-dark of the Rocky Mountains. She didn't want to answer.

Chapter Ten

Sean was familiar with most of Emily's tactics when it came to arguments. When she didn't answer him back right away, her silence meant she was hiding something. He sank into the plush chair opposite hers. He didn't want to fight. They were on a private jet headed toward one of the most romantic cities in the world, and he hadn't completely ruled out the possibility of inducting her into the Mile High Club.

But he couldn't leave Paco the Pimp hanging. Apparently this Paco had been a passenger on Wynter's deluxe yacht. "You've told me about the night of the murder. You claimed you were at a yacht party. True or false?"

"True."

He poured the wine, a half glass for her and the same for himself. "But you never told me how you got an invite to this insider party. I'm guessing it had something to do with Paco the Pimp. True or false?"

"I don't want to talk about this."

"And I know why," he said. "Your pal Paco was invited to provide a bunch of party girls for the guys on the yacht. And you convinced him to take you along. You went undercover."

"Fine," she snapped. "You're right. I was all dolled up in a sparkly skintight dress, four-inch heels and gobs of heavy makeup."

"A hooker disguise."

"Sleazy except for my long hair. I had it pinned up on top of my head when I went there. I thought it was sophisticated." She sipped her wine. "Paco said I should wear it down. He thought the men would like it."

Imagining her being ogled in a sexy dress made his blood boil. Of course they liked her long, beautiful hair. "What the hell, Emily? You used to believe that hiding your identity was dishonest and unfair."

"You've got no room to talk," she said. "You used to go undercover all the time."

"And you never approved."

"Maybe not."

"And I was trained for it. I have certain traits and abilities that lend themselves to undercover work, namely, I'm good at deception." He downed his wine in two glugs. "You're not like that. You're a lousy liar."

"I've changed. I know when to keep my mouth shut instead of blurting out the truth. I can be circumspect."

"You can't change your basic nature," he said as he poured more wine. "Undercover work is not your thing."

"I pulled it off on Wynter's yacht."

He glared at her. "Not a shining example of a successful mission."

"I made mistakes," she admitted. "Okay, all right, it was gross. Witnessing the murder was the worst, but being pawed by sleazeballs was bad. One of them grabbed me by my hair and kissed me. Another patted my hair like I was a dog. The very next day, I went to the beauty shop and told them to cut it off."

"You're never going to go undercover again, understand?"

"Don't tell me what I can and can't do."

Through clenched teeth, he said, "I'm sorry."

She looked at him as though he'd sprouted petunias from the top of his head. "Did I hear you correctly?"

"You're right. I can't tell you what to do. However, if you decide to go undercover again, I want to know. Give me a chance to show you how to do it without getting yourself killed."

"My turn to apologize," she said. "You're also right. I had no business waltzing onto that yacht without the proper training. The only reason I got out of there in one piece was dumb luck."

He held up his plastic glass to salute her. The wine he'd already inhaled was taking the sharp edge off, but he was still alert enough to realize that something significant had occurred: they hadn't gotten into a fight.

Both of them had been ticked off. They'd danced around the volcano, but neither had erupted. Instead, they'd talked like adults and settled their differences. Maybe she'd matured. Maybe he'd gotten more sensitive. *Whatever!* He'd gladly settle for this fragile truce instead of gut-wrenching hostility.

He didn't want to discuss their successful handling of the problem for fear that he'd jinx the positive mood. What had they been talking about before takeoff? Oh yeah, the agenda for their time in San Francisco. He wanted to take her to dinner at the Italian restaurant where he proposed.

He gazed toward her. She looked youthful but not too young. Had she changed in the past five years? If he looked closely, he could see fine lines at the corners of her turquoise eyes, and her features seemed sharper, more honed. With her black sweater covering her torso, he could only guess how her body had changed. A vision of her nicely proportioned shoulders, round breasts and slender waist was easy to recall. He hadn't forgotten the constellation of freckles across her back or the tattoo of a cute little rodent above her left breast that she referred to as a "titmouse."

Since he wasn't allowed to touch her without disobeying half a dozen of their weird ground rules, he had to stop thinking like this. Her unapproachable nearness would drive him mad. Back to business, back to the investigation, he said, "Tomorrow, our first appointment should be a meeting with Levine to see if the FBI has any new info."

"But not at the fed office," she reminded him. "Dylan thinks their phones are bugged."

He considered it unlikely that Levine was working with Wynter, but Sean didn't want to take any chances. "I'd rather not let him know where we're staying. We'll meet him for breakfast."

"After that," she said, "we should go to Chinatown. I had a couple of leads there, and I'd like to talk to Doris Liu again. She's the woman who took in Roger Patrone and raised him."

He'd almost forgotten that Patrone was an orphan who had been taken in by a family in Chinatown. "There must have been something remarkable about Patrone when he was a kid. Most residents in Chinatown aren't welcoming to strangers."

"It's been hard for me to ask around," she said. "Patrone's gambling operation—last I heard it was a stud poker game, Texas Hold'em and two blackjack tables—is in the rear of a strip club in the Tenderloin. Even with the attempts at gentrification, I don't blend in."

The Tenderloin had earned its reputation as a high-crime district. He was deeply grateful that she hadn't tried an undercover stint as a stripper. "I'll go there, no problem."

"And I wouldn't mind sneaking onto Wynter's yacht and looking around."

Breaking and entering didn't appeal to him, but he definitely liked the idea of getting out on the water in the bay. San Francisco had many charms, ranging from unique architecture to culture to amazing restaurants. The best, he thought, were the piers and the ocean...the scent of salt water...the whisper of the surf.

She yawned. "Maybe we should go to the docks. I only tried to get in there once, and it didn't go well. The guys who work with shipping containers ignored me, and the supervisors were overly polite, thinking I was sent by management to check up on them."

"What can we learn there?"

"I'm not sure," she said. "It's another avenue."

They were going to be busy. "Tired?"

"A bit," she said.

"You can take off your seat belt and lie on the sofa. It folds out into a bed."

She peeked out the porthole. "How long before we're in San Francisco?"

"A couple of hours." The flight time on commercial airlines was two and a half hours. The Gulfstream took a little longer.

"I wouldn't mind a catnap," she said.

He moved their wineglasses to cup holders beside the chairs, picked up the nearly empty wine bottle and tucked away the table. Before he transformed the sofa into a bed, he opened a storage compartment and took out a thermal blanket and a pillow. Then he dimmed the lights.

After fluffing the pillow, she stood and fidgeted beside the sofa bed. "I feel selfish, taking the only bed. You're as tired as I am."

"Is that an invitation to join you?"

"No," she said softly. "Sorry, I didn't mean to give you that idea."

Her tone sounded regretful. If he pushed, he might be able to change her mind. But now wasn't the right time. He didn't want to rock the boat while they were in a fairly good place. At least they weren't fighting. It was best not to complicate things with sex. *Great sex*, he reminded himself. They'd always had great sex.

"Not tonight," he said, as much to himself as to her. "Lie down. I'm going up to the cockpit."

"With the other cocks?"

"You might say that." He wouldn't, but she would.

No matter how much she claimed to be a responsible, sober adult, there was a goofball just below the surface. That was the Emily that drove him crazy, the Emily he loved.

WHILE SHE SLEPT, Sean spent time with his buddy David and the copilot. He loved the night view from the cockpit with stars scattered across the sky. He felt like they were part of the galaxies.

They talked, and he made coffee to counteract the slight inebriation he'd felt. A professional bodyguard shouldn't be drinking on the job, but he couldn't pretend that this was a standard assignment.

If she'd been anyone else, he would have advised them to leave the investigating to the police. And if they refused, he would have terminated the contract. Not a detective, he was well aware that he didn't have the resources that were available to him when he was in the FBI. On the other hand, he had the hacking skills of his brother and none of those pesky restrictions.

Finally, he was peering through the clouds and wispy curtains of fog to see the lights of San Francisco, and he felt a surge. His pulse sped up. His blood pumped harder. This city was the setting for the best time in his life and the absolute, rock-bottom worst. Emily was intrinsic to both.

He went back to the cabin and found her lying on her side, spooning the pillow. As soon as he touched her shoulder, she wakened.

"I'm up," she said, throwing off the blanket.

"Almost there. You need to put on a seat belt."

"Do I have time to splash water on my face?"

"Okay, if you hurry."

While she darted into the bathroom, he verified their arrangements on his phone. They had a suite reserved at the Pendragon Hotel and there should be a rental car waiting at the private airfield. Sean wanted to believe they'd be safe, at least for tonight, but his gut told him to watch for trouble. He put in a call to Dylan at the TST office.

"We're here," Sean announced, purposely not naming the city in case somebody was listening. "Anything to report?"

"Wynter must be taking advantage of his location near Silicon Valley and hiring top-notch programmers. His security is state-of-the-art, truly hard to hack."

Oddly, Dylan sounded happy. Sean asked, "You like the challenge?"

"Oh yeah. Getting through these firewalls will be an accomplishment."

"I'll leave you to it."

"Hang on a sec. I had a phone call from your new BFF, Morelli. He wanted to make an information exchange."

"What did you tell him?"

"I said you'd call him back."

"Thanks, bro."

He disconnected the call. Morelli's business

card with all his numbers was burning a hole in his pocket. Though Sean was tempted to make the call, he'd warned Morelli not to contact him. It might seem weak to call back. But it was possible that Morelli had useful information.

Sean set the scrambler on his phone so he couldn't be traced and punched in the numbers for Morelli's cell phone. As soon as the other man answered, he said, "What do you want?"

"Let me talk to Emily."

"You're wasting my time," Sean said. "Talk."

"Tell her that she's not going to be able to sell her articles to the *BP Reporter* anymore. That's one of the places she published her last article on Wynter."

"Why can't she sell there?"

"A terrible accident happened in their office. The police are saying a leak in the gas main resulted in the fiery explosion that destroyed the building."

"Any deaths or injuries?"

"The editor is in the hospital." Morelli paused for a moment. "It's fortunate that Emily wasn't there."

Chapter Eleven

Any complacency Emily had been feeling vanished when Sean told her of the explosion. *BP Reporter* was a giveaway newspaper filled with shopping specials and coupons, and the pay for articles was next to nothing. Most writers saw *BP*, which stood for Blog/Print, as a stepping-stone to actual paying assignments. The editor, Jerome Strauss, wasn't a close friend, but she knew him and she felt guilty about his injuries. She was to blame. There wasn't a doubt in her mind that Wynter was behind the supposed "gas leak" detonation.

Refreshed from her catnap and energized by righteous rage, she found it difficult to wait until they got to the Pendragon Hotel to start her inquiries. They'd gained an hour traveling to the West Coast. It was after two o'clock in the morning when they entered the suite.

She set up her laptop on a desk in the living

room and watched while Sean prowled through the suite with his gun held ready. The floor plan for the suite was open space with the kitchen delineated by a counter and the bedroom separated by a half wall and an arch. Sean was thorough, peering into closets and looking under the bed. When he was apparently satisfied that there were no bad guys lurking, he unpacked some strange equipment. One piece looked like an extension rod for selfies.

"What's that?" she asked.

"An all-purpose sweeper to locate bugs, hidden cameras and the like."

Though she appreciated his attention to detail, she didn't understand why it was needed. "How would anybody know we were coming to this hotel and were assigned to this room?"

"I've stayed here before. And I asked for this room. It's on the top floor, the sixth. Since this is the tallest building on the block, it's hard for anybody with a telescope or a sniper rifle to take aim. There's a nice view when the fog lifts."

"It's a nice hotel," she agreed. The exterior was classic San Francisco architecture, and the furnishings were clean lined, Asian inspired. "Why would there be bugs?"

"I want to be sure we're safe." He started waving his long camera thingy, scanning the room for electronic devices. "Get used to this, Emily. From now on, I'm hyperprotective."

Tempted to make a snarky comment about how vigilance sometimes crossed the line into obsessive-compulsive disorder, she kept her lip zipped. He was the expert, and she needed to rely on his judgment. She sauntered across the room to the counter that separated the kitchenette and climbed onto a stool. "I need to start making phone calls. Which phone should I use?"

"It depends on who you're calling."

"How so?"

He explained, "If you're talking to somebody suspicious who might try to track your location, use the secure phone Dylan gave you. If it's somebody you feel safe with, use a burner. We can load up a burner and pitch it."

He seemed to be thinking of all contingencies. "I want to track down Strauss by calling hospitals."

"Burner," he said as he continued to sweep the room.

She called four hospitals before she found the right one. The only information the on-duty nurse would give her was that Strauss was in "fair" condition, but not allowed to have visitors, especially not visitors from the press.

Relieved but not completely satisfied, she wished she had the type of access the FBI and SFPD had. It didn't seem fair. Law enforcement officers wouldn't be barred from the room, but the press—the very people Strauss worked with every day—had to take a step back.

If Strauss was awake, she'd bet he was planning his coverage on the explosion. The story had fallen into his lap. Would he let her be the one to write about it?

She wasn't his favorite reporter. He knew her as Emily, and she submitted only puff pieces, but the explosion might be a way to integrate her real identity with her secret pseudonym. Strauss already did business with her fake persona; the article about Wynter had been published first by an online news journal that paid for her investigative skills. Strauss had permission for a reprint that cost him nothing.

Maybe she could get Sean to use his influence with Agent Levine to sneak her into the hospital room. She went into the bedroom area behind Japanese-style screens to ask.

There were two full-size beds, and he had taken the one nearer to the archway connecting bedroom and living room. He'd pulled back the spread and collapsed onto the sheets. His shoes were off, but he still wore his jeans and T-shirt. In repose, his features relaxed, and he seemed almost innocent. She crept up beside him and turned off the globe-shaped lamp on the bedside table.

Before she could tiptoe out of the room, his hand shot out and grasped her wrist. His movement was unexpected. She gasped loudly and struggled to pull away from him. He held on more tightly. "Turn it back on."

"I wanted to make it dark so you could sleep."

"Can't see an intruder." He hadn't opened his eyes. "Leave the light on."

She flicked the switch, he released his grasp and she scuttled into the front room with her heart beating fast. He'd startled her, and her fear was close to the surface. If he could spook her so easily, how was she going to fall asleep?

If she stayed up, what could she do? It was too early to make phone calls, and she wanted to talk to Dylan before she used the laptop so she wouldn't accidentally trigger any alarms.

A sigh pushed through her lips. Lying down on the bed was probably a good idea. Getting herself cleaned up was next best.

The huge bathroom was mostly white marble with caramel streaks. Fluffy white towels in varying sizes sat on open shelving that went floor to ceiling. She wasn't really a bathtub person, and the glassed-in shower enticed her.

For a full half hour, Emily indulged herself. Steaming hot water from four different jets sluiced over her body. The sandalwood fragrance of the soap permeated her skin, and she washed her hair with floral-scented shampoo while humming the song about San Francisco and flowers in her hair.

She toweled dry, styled her hair with a blow-dryer and slipped into a sleeveless nightshirt that fell to her knees. Before leaving the bathroom, she turned out the light so she wouldn't disturb Sean.

After she pulled down her covers, she glanced over at his sleeping form. Under the sheets, he stretched out the full length of the bed on his back with his arms folded on his chest. His eyes were closed. He'd stripped off his clothes and appeared to be naked, which had always been his preferred way to sleep.

When they were married, she'd always looked forward to those nights when she was already in bed, not quite asleep and waiting for him. He'd enter the room quietly and slip under the covers, and she'd realize that he was completely naked. She remembered the heat radiating from his big, hard, masculine body, and when he'd pulled her into his arms, she was warmed to the marrow of her bones.

The pattern of hair on his chest reminded her of those days, long ago. Her fingers itched to touch him. She sat on the edge of her bed, silently hoping that he'd open his eyes and ask her to come closer.

Their ground rules started with the obvious: no falling in love, followed by no public display of affection. The complicated part was initiating contact. If he went first, he had to ask. But she was free to pounce on him at any time. *What am I waiting for?*

She shifted position, sitting lightly on his bed and watching him for any sign that he was awake. The steady rise and fall of his chest indicated that he hadn't noticed her nearness. Maybe she'd steal a kiss and return to her own bed.

She leaned down closer. Her heart thumped faster. Her entire body trembled with anticipation. Falling in love with her ex-husband was completely out of the question. If anything happened between them, she couldn't expect it to mean anything. *Really? Am I capable of having sex without love?*

A couple of times in the past, she'd engaged in meaningless sex. The result was never good, hardly worth the effort. Maybe that type of sex would be blah with Sean, but she doubted it. He was too skillful, and he knew exactly which buttons to punch with her. The real question was: Did she dare to open herself up to him, knowing that he'd broken her heart and fearing that he might do it again?

A scary possibility, too scary. She was too much of a coward to take the risk. Exhaling a sigh of sad regret, she pulled away from him, turned her head and stood.

"Emily?"

"Yes."

He was out of the bed, standing beside her.

She glided into his embrace, and he positioned her against his naked body. They fit together like yin and yang, like spaghetti and meatballs, like Tarzan and Jane. *Take me, Lord of the Jungle!* She was becoming hysterical. If she was going to avoid sex, she'd better stop him now.

His kiss sent her reeling. With very little effort, he'd caught her.

All logic vanished. The pleasure of his touch erased conscious thought. All she wanted was to savor each sensation. He pressed more firmly against her. She couldn't fight him, didn't want to. *If this is what sex without love feels like, sign me up.*

He gathered the hem of her nightshirt in his hands. Looking down, he read the message on the front. "Promote Literacy. Kiss a Poet."

"I'm just doing my bit to promote education."

"Noble," he said.

In a single gesture, he lifted the nightshirt up and over her head. Underneath, she was as nude as he. By the light of the bedside lamp, her gaze slid appreciatively downward, from his shoulders to the dusting of chest hair to his muscular abs and lower. He was even more flawless than she remembered.

"Hey, lady." He lifted her chin. "My eyes are up here."

"And they're very nice eyes, very dark chocolate and hot. At the moment, however—" she gave him a wicked smile "—I'm more interested in a different part of your body."

He scooped her off her feet and dove with her onto the bed. With great energy, he flung off the covers, plumped pillows and settled her in place before he straddled her hips.

For a moment, she lay motionless below him. She just stared at her magnificent ex-husband. Sex always brought out the poet in her. *He was her knight errant, her Lancelot, a conquering hero who would plunder and ravage her.* Which made her…what? Surely not a helpless maiden; she drove her own destiny. And she most certainly would not lie passively while he had all the fun.

Struggling, she sat up enough to grab his arms and pull him toward her. *A futile effort.* He was in control, and he let her know it by pinning her wrists on either side of her head. He was too strong. She couldn't fight him.

"Relax, Emily." His baritone rumbled through her. "Let me take care of you."

She wriggled. "Maybe you could speed it up."

"I've thought about this for a long time." He dropped a kiss on her forehead. "I want it to last for a very long time."

He hovered over her, balancing on his elbows and his knees. In contrast to his flurry of activity, he slowly lowered himself, seeming to float inches above her. Their lips touched. His chest grazed the tips of her breasts.

She arched her back, desperate to join her flesh with his. He wrestled her down, forcing her to experience each feather touch separately. Shivers of pleasure shot through her, setting off a mad, convulsive reaction that rattled from the ends of her hair to the soles of her feet. She threw her head back against the pillow. Her toes curled.

"Now, Sean. I want you, please."

"Good things are…worth the wait."

His seduction was slow and deliberate, driving her crazy. Her lungs throbbed. She breathed hoarsely, panting and gasping as a wave of pleasure rolled over her. Oh God, she'd missed this! The way he handled her, manipulating her so she felt deeply and passionately. Transformed, she was aware of her own sexuality.

"You're a goddess," he whispered.

And she felt like some kind of superior being who was beautiful, brilliant and powerful. If she could be like this in everyday life, Emily would rule the world.

Somehow, magically, they changed positions and she was on top. She kissed his neck, inhaling his musky scent and tasting the salty flavor of his flesh. She bit down. He was yummy, a full meal.

He nudged her away from his throat. "Did you turn into a vampire or are you just giving me a hickey?"

"I'll be a sultry vampire." She raked her fingers through the hair on his chest. "And you can be a wolf man."

"I like it."

"Me, too."

Sex with Sean was a full-contact sport, engaging mind and body, mostly body, though. He teased and cajoled and fondled and kissed and nibbled.

She'd missed the great sex that only Sean could give her. Not that it was all his doing. She played her part—the role of a goddess—in their crazy, wild affection. And when she reached her earth-shaking climax, she came completely undone, disassembled. It felt like she'd actually left her body and soared to the stratosphere. When she came back to earth, she couldn't wait to do it again.

So they did. Twice more that night.

Chapter Twelve

The next morning, Sean lifted his eyelids and scanned the open-space suite at the Pendragon Hotel. Yesterday might have been the longest day of his life with more ups and downs than a roller coaster, but he wasn't complaining. The day had turned out great. Sex with Emily was even better than he'd remembered. Their chemistry was incredible. No other woman came close.

He gazed at her, sleeping beside him. She was on her stomach, and the sheet had slipped down, revealing a partial view of her smooth, creamy white bottom. He wanted to see more. Carefully, so he wouldn't wake her, he caught the sheet between two fingers and tugged.

Immediately, she reached back to swat his hand away. She peered through a tangle of hair as she rolled to her side and rearranged the sheet to cover her lovely round breasts. *A bit late for mod-*

esty, he thought, but he said nothing. He wanted another bout of sex, and he was fairly sure she was ready for more of the same.

"Time?" she asked.

He stretched his neck so he could see the decorative clock on the bedside table. The combination of chrome circles and squares showed the time in the upper-left corner.

"Eight forty-six." He looked past the archway into the living room, where faint light appeared around the shades. "The sun's up."

"I thought we were going to run out the door early and have breakfast with Levine."

"It'll have to be brunch. Maybe even lunch." He made a grab for her, but she evaded him. "About last night..."

"Enough said." She climbed out of bed with the sheet wrapped around her. "I'm glad we got that out of the way."

She made wonderful sex sound like a distasteful chore. Surely he'd heard her wrong. "Are you talking about us? You and me? About what happened last night?"

"It was just sex."

"Sure, and Everest is just a mountain. The Lamborghini is just a car."

"The tension was building between us, and we had to relieve it. That's what last night was about." With one hand, she clutched the sheet while the other rubbed the sleep out of her eyes. "I promise you—it's never going to happen again."

She pivoted, squared her shoulders and marched into the bathroom while he sat on the bed, gaping as he watched her hasty retreat. *Never going to happen again?* He'd be damned if he believed her. She might as well tell the birds not to sing and the fish not to swim. He could not deny his nature, and his inner voice told him to have sex with her as soon and as often as possible.

His number one job, however, was keeping her safe, and meeting with Special Agent Greg Levine was a good place to start. Sean decided not to make the phone call to set the time and the place until he and Emily were near the restaurant; he didn't want Levine to have time to plan ahead.

After they were dressed, he gave her a glance, pretending not to notice how tiny her waist looked in the belted slacks that hugged her bottom. He stared pointedly at her flat ballet shoes. "Do you have sneakers?"

"They don't exactly go with this outfit." She slipped on the matching gray jacket to the pantsuit. "I want to look professional to meet with Levine, and my suitcase is packed with outdoorsy stuff for Colorado."

"You need to wear running shoes. Obvious reasons."

"Okay." She exhaled a little sigh. "Anything else?"

"A hooded sweatshirt?"

"Don't have one with me. I've got several at my apartment. Can we swing past there?"

She wasn't actually disagreeing with him, but her reluctance to follow his instructions was annoying. "Don't you get it? These guys want to kill you. If they recognize you, you're dead."

Her full lips pinched together. "If we can figure out a way to go to my apartment, I have a couple of already-made disguises to go with my pseudonyms. There's a really good one that makes me look like a guy."

Impossible!

He turned away from her and went to the kitchenette to fill his coffee mug again. "Try to find something that makes you look anonymous. Wynter's men might be following Levine."

When she emerged from the bedroom, she threw her arms wide and announced her presence. "Ta-da! Do I look like a punk kid from the city streets?"

Without makeup, her face looked about fourteen. But her jeans were too well fitted. And her Berkeley sweatshirt looked almost new. "Not a street kid," he said. "You look more like a cheerleader."

"Is that anonymous enough?"

"Still too cute. Men will notice you." He motioned for her to come closer. "Give me the sweatshirt."

In one of the kitchen drawers, he found a pair of heavy scissors, which he used to whack off the arms on the sweatshirt and to make a long slit down from the collar. He turned it inside out and tossed it back to her.

"You ruined my sweatshirt," she said as she pulled it over her head. Underneath, she wore a blue blouse with long sleeves. "How's this?"

"Better, but I still can't erase your prettiness." He tilted his head to the side for a different perspective. "Maybe we should cut off the jeans."

"I'd rather not. These cost almost two hundred bucks."

He stalked into the bedroom, dug around in his backpack and took out two baseball caps. The one that was worse for wear, he gave to her. "Whenever you go outside, wear this. It won't change your appearance, but it hides your face."

His clothes were more nondescript than hers; people tended not to notice a guy in jeans, T-shirt and plaid flannel overshirt. If he stooped his shoulders a bit to disguise his height, he'd fade into almost any background.

They left the hotel shortly after ten o'clock, late enough that the morning fog had lifted. When he'd been living in San Francisco, he had a hard time adjusting to fog. Sunny days in Denver numbered about 245 a year, and when it was sunny the sky was open and blue. Sean came to think of the morning fog as the day waking slowly, reticent to leave nighttime dreams behind.

This was the city where he first fell in love with Emily, and he saw the buildings, neighborhoods and streets through rose-colored glasses. If last night's sensuality had been allowed to grow and flourish, he would have felt the same today, but she'd squashed his mood.

Behind the wheel of his rental car, he asked, "Is that North Beach café with the great coffee still there?"

"You mean Henny's," she said. "It's there and the coffee is still yummy."

The location wasn't particularly convenient to the FBI offices near Golden Gate Park, but Sean wasn't planning to go easy on his former coworker. The best explanation for how Wynter found out about Emily was that Levine was incompetent enough to get his phone tapped and not know it. At worst, he was working with Wynter.

There was street parking outside Henny's Café, a corner eatery with a fat red hen for a logo. He found a place halfway down the block and parallel parked. He ordered her to stay in the car while he did swift reconnaissance inside the café, which was only half-full and had a good view of the street and an exit into the alley.

Back in the car, he called Levine. The trick to this phone call would be to keep from mentioning Emily or Wynter or the possibility that the FBI phones were tapped.

After the initial hello, Sean said, "Long time no see, buddy. Do you remember that case we worked? With the twins who kept spying on each other?"

"Uh-huh, I remember." Levine sounded confused.

"The big thing in that case has been getting more and more common." Sean's reference was to wiretapping, which had been the key to solving the twin case. "Have you ever had a problem like that?"

"What are you getting at?"

"It's probably nothing. I just hope you aren't infected…" *With a bug on your phone.* "Know what I mean?"

"Damn right I do." His confusion was replaced with anger. As a rule, feds don't like having somebody outside the agency tell them that their phones aren't secure. "What about that other matter? The problem with—"

"The Em agenda," Sean said. "Meet me, within the hour, and we'll talk."

After he rattled off the name of the restaurant

and the address, he ended the call and turned to Emily, who had been patiently, quietly waiting.

"He'll be here," he said. "We'll wait in the car until he shows up."

"Did you refer to me as the Em agenda?"

"To avoid saying your name."

"Cool, like a code name." She was off and running, chattering on about how she could be a spy. "Just call me Agent Em."

She needed to understand that they weren't playing a fantasy espionage game. The danger was real. But when Emily followed one of her tangents, she was bright and charming and impossible to resist.

When they were married, it was one of the things he had loved about her. He could sit back and listen to her riff about some oddball topic. She called it free verse; he called it adorable.

"Hold on," he said. "I'm still mad."

"About what?"

"You gave me the brush-off this morning."

"Didn't mean to upset you," she said. "We had an agreement, ground rules. I'm just making sure I don't fall in love with you again."

"There's a difference between sex and love."

"Well, listen to you." Her eyebrows lifted. "Aren't you surprisingly sensitive?"

"I told you I've changed."

"You hardly seem like the same guy who took me to a Forty-Niners game at Levi's Stadium and got in a shouting match that almost came to blows."

"They insulted my Broncos," he said.

"Heaven forbid."

The near fistfight at the football game hadn't been his finest hour, but the undercover work had been eating away at him. He'd needed to let off steam. "I know there were times when I was hard to live with."

"Me, too," she said. "Let's keep it in the past. And never fall in love again."

"As long as we agree that not falling in love doesn't mean we can't have sex."

"That's a deal."

When she held out her hand to shake on the agreement, he yanked her closer and gave her a kiss. He caught her in the middle of a gasp, but her mouth was pliant. Soon she was kissing him back. Emily's recently logical brain might be opposed to sex, but her body hadn't gotten the message. She wanted him as much as he wanted her.

When he turned away and looked out the windshield, he spied Special Agent Greg Levine crossing the street and heading toward Henny's. Walking fast and staring down at the cell phone in his hand, Levine gave off the vibe of a stressed-out businessman and had the wardrobe to match: dark gray suit, blue shirt and necktie tugged loose. His dark blond hair was trimmed in much the same style as Sean's but wasn't as thick. The strands across the front were working hard to cover his forehead.

As Sean escorted Emily up the sidewalk to the café, she asked, "Is there anything I should be careful of saying or not saying? You know, in case Levine isn't on our side."

"Don't mention Hazel. Definitely don't mention that Dylan might hack in to his system." Until they knew otherwise, Sean would treat Levine like an ally instead of an enemy. "First I'm going to pump him to find out how Wynter learned there was a witness. And then how he knew the witness was you."

"I want to ask him what the FBI knows about Patrone's family in Chinatown, the people who took him in when he was a kid."

He nodded. "Anything else?"

"It goes without saying that I want to see if Levine can get me into the hospital to see Strauss."

Inside Henny's, they joined Levine in a cantaloupe-orange leatherette booth at the back. Henny's specialized mostly in breakfast and lunch. The decor was chipper with sunlight filtering through the storefront windows, dozens of cutouts and pictures of chickens and a counter surrounded by swivel stools. A cozy place to wake up, and yet they served alcohol.

Sean did a handshake and half hug with Levine. They'd worked together but never had been close. Since Sean worked undercover, he was seldom in the office; the only agent he cared about was his handler/supervisor, and he knew she'd returned to Quantico. He listened while Levine updated him on other people they knew in common.

The waitress returned to their table with a Bloody Mary for Levine. He must have ordered when he walked in the door. Vodka before noon; not a good sign. Remembering her preference, Sean ordered a cappuccino for Emily. He wanted a double espresso.

"You and Emily," Levine said with a knowing grin. "I always thought you two would get back together."

"We're not together," Emily said. "I hired Sean to act as my bodyguard."

"You're his boss? The one who cracks the whip?" His grin turned into a full-on smirk. "I underestimated you, girl."

"Don't call her girl," Sean said coldly. "And yeah, you didn't give her enough credit. I haven't seen your files, but she's got enough on Wynter for an arrest."

"I'm working on it." Levine swizzled the celery in his glass before he raised it to his lips. "I've got a snitch on the inside."

Sean hadn't expected him to be so forthcoming. As long as Levine was being talkative, he asked, "How did Wynter find out there was a witness to Patrone's murder?"

"The murder was investigated by the SFPD. Patrone was a known associate of Wynter, which put suspicion off Wynter. At first, they investigated Wynter's rivals."

Sean didn't need a history of the crime. "But they came around to the real story. How did that happen?"

Levine couldn't meet his gaze. Dark smudges under his eyes made Sean think he wasn't sleeping well. His chin quivered as he attempted to change the direction of their conversation. "Why do you think my phone is bugged?"

"Simple logic. There's no reason for anybody to connect Emily to me. We haven't seen or talked to each other since the divorce. But you called my office in Denver—"

"I told you," Levine said. "I always thought the two of you would get back together. Hell, you're the reason Emily showed up on our doorstep instead of going to the police. She knew us because of you."

He looked to Emily for confirmation. "Is that true?"

"I thought the FBI would be more careful about keeping my identity secret."

Anger heated Sean's blood. She should have been able to trust the feds, but they'd been sloppy. He glared at Levine. "Did you tell them about Emily?"

"I had to give them something. The cops were off base, asking questions that riled other gangs." His voice held a note of believable desperation. "I said there was a witness and leaked her account of the murder. But I didn't give her name."

Assessing his behavioral cues, Sean deduced that Levine was honestly sorry about the way things had turned out. He'd never meant to put Emily in danger. "I believe you."

"Damn right you do." Levine nodded vigorously. His relief was palpable. "You would have done the same thing."

"I don't think so." Sean didn't allow him to get comfortable. "There are other ways to play a witness, but I'm not here to give you a lesson. You asked why I suspected a wiretap on your phone."

"Right."

"After you called my office, one of Wynter's men made the same contact. How would they know about me if they weren't monitoring your phone?"

Levine took another drink. His Bloody Mary was almost gone, and he ordered another when the waitress brought their coffee drinks. Sean and Emily also ordered breakfast. Levine didn't want food.

While the waitress bustled back to the kitchen,

Levine leaned across the table on his elbows and asked, "Did you talk to the guy Wynter sent?"

Sean nodded. "John Morelli."

Levine bolted upright in the booth. It looked like he'd been poked by a cattle prod. "Morelli is my snitch."

Chapter Thirteen

Emily twisted her hands together in her lap as though she could somehow physically hold things together. Nothing made sense anymore. Morelli was her contact but also a snitch, and then he'd pulled a gun on Sean, which made him an enemy. The more Levine talked, the more confounded she felt. Had Morelli been lying to Sean when he said he only wanted to talk to her? He'd said she had information about who was stealing from Wynter. It might be important to go through her notes and figure out what he meant.

While Sean and Levine talked about Morelli, trying to figure out if he could be trusted, she pulled her cap lower on her forehead and slouched down in the booth. How was she ever going to make sense of this tangled mess? Maybe Sean had been right when he suggested leaving town and forgetting all about Wynter and human trafficking. She could retract her witness statement and start her life over.

But she couldn't ignore her conscience, and, somewhere in the back of her mind, she imagined the ghost of the murdered man haunting her. She owed it to him to bring his killer to justice.

She spoke up, "It seems like everybody knows I'm the witness. I should just go to the SFPD."

"Makes sense," Sean said. "And that's ultimately what you'll have to do. But right now we're flying under the radar. Let's take advantage of the moment."

"Where do we start?"

"If we figure out why Patrone was murdered, it takes the focus off you."

Similar ideas had been spinning through her mind, but he pulled it together and made perfect sense. Why was Patrone killed? What was the motive?

After the waitress delivered their breakfast, Emily took a bite of her omelet and looked over at Levine. "You might be able to help us."

"What do you need?"

"More background data on Roger Patrone. I know about the gambling operation in the strip club. And I know the woman who took him into her home is Doris Liu." Emily had visited her once and gotten a big, fat, "No comment" in hostile Cantonese. "Patrone must have had other friends and associates outside Wynter's operation."

"He almost married a woman who owns a tourist shop in Chinatown on Grant. Her name is Liane Zhou. Nobody bothers her because her brother, Mikey Zhou, is said to be a snakehead."

Emily shuddered. The snakeheads were notorious gangsters who smuggled people into the country. "Does Mikey Zhou work with Wynter's people?"

"Their businesses overlap."

"If you can call crime a business," she said.

"Hell, yes, it's a business."

"A filthy business."

Her own fears and doubts seemed minor in comparison to these larger crimes. Tearing people away from their homes and forcing them into a life of prostitution or slave labor horrified her. According to her research, parents in poverty-stricken villages sometimes sold their children to the snakeheads, thinking their kids might achieve a better life in a different country. Others signed up with the snakeheads to escape persecution at home.

"Human smuggling is a complex job," Levine said as he carefully smoothed the thinning hair across his forehead. "They need ledgers and accounting methods to track how many have been taken and how they're transported. Most often, it's in shipping containers. Then they have to determine how many arrived, how they'll be dispersed and the final payout for delivery. But you know that—don't you, Emily? Isn't that why you were on Wynter's yacht in the first place? You intended to steal his computer records and ledgers."

"So what?" She hadn't actually told him about her plan to download Wynter's personal computer, but it wasn't a stretch for him to figure it out.

"Did you get the download you were looking for?"

She'd failed. After Frankie and the boys had cleared out of the office, she had spent the rest of the night running and hiding. But she didn't want to share that information with Levine. There was something about him that she didn't trust. "The only thing that matters is stopping Wynter. How can we disrupt his business?"

"Cut into his profit," Sean said. "But that won't work as long as there's a market for what he's selling."

"It's slavery," she said. "Twenty-first-century slavery. And it's wrong. How can people justify the buying and selling of human beings?"

"Don't be naive," Levine said. "People argue that prostitutes are a necessary vice. And slave labor keeps production costs down. The freaking founding fathers owned slaves. It took a civil war to change our ideas."

She glanced between Levine and Sean. The FBI agent thought she was a wide-eyed innocent who had no clue about the real world. Her ex-husband had told her dozens of times that she was unrealistic and immature. But those complaints were years ago. Sean was different now.

Looking him straight in the eye, she said, "It's our responsibility as decent human beings to expose these crimes and disrupt this network of evil and depravity."

Levine chuckled. "That sounds like a good lead for one of your articles."

"Sounds like the truth," Sean said.

"Do you really think so?" she asked.

"I've always tried to be a responsible man."

A man she could love. She bit her lower lip. *Don't say it, don't.* After the divorce, she'd wondered how two people who were so unlike each other could be attracted. What had she ever seen in him?

This was her answer. At his core, Sean was decent, trustworthy and, yes, responsible. He was a good man.

She straightened her posture and dug into her breakfast. If she was going to save the world, she needed fuel in her system. Listening with half an ear, she heard Sean and Levine discussing lines of communication that wouldn't compromise Sean's location and would make Wynter think his wiretap at the FBI was still operational.

"Then there's Morelli," Sean said. "Can you use your snitch to feed bad information to Wynter?"

"He wasn't always lying to me," Levine said. He fussed with his hair and finished his second Bloody Mary. "I made a couple of arrests based on intel he gave me."

"You can't trust him," Sean said firmly. "Get that through your head. Morelli isn't your pal."

Emily felt Sean's temperature rising. He was getting angry, and she didn't blame him. Levine was beginning to slur, and his eyelids drooped to half-mast.

Before Sean blew his top, she needed information from Levine. "What can you tell me about Jerome Strauss?"

"The editor of *BP*? He's fine, already out of the hospital."

Good news, finally! She waved her hands. "Yay."

"Strauss is one lucky bastard. He'd fallen asleep at the office and just happened to wake up a few minutes before the bomb—which was on a timer—went off. Strauss was in the bathroom when it exploded. The EMTs found him wandering around with no pants."

"So he wasn't badly hurt?"

"If he'd been in the office near the window, he'd be dead. All he had were some bruises and a minor concussion. Lucky, lucky, lucky."

Or not. Emily enjoyed fairy tales about pots of gold at the end of the rainbow and genies in lamps who granted three wishes, but life wasn't like that. There were few real coincidences. Strauss had escaped, and she was glad but…but also suspicious. He might have been complicit in blowing up his own office.

While she and Sean dug into their food, Levine scooted to the edge of the booth. "I should get back to work," he said. "I can't say it's been great to see you."

"Same here," Sean said.

"If I can be of help, let me know." He gave a wave and whipped out the door, obviously glad to be leaving them behind.

She watched him lurch down the street. He stumbled at the curb. "He's about three months away from getting a toupee."

"I didn't remember him as being so nervous." Sean sopped up the last bit of syrup with his pancake. "The FBI in SF has gone downhill since I left."

She nudged his shoulder. "I'll bet you were the best fed since…who's a famous FBI agent?"

"Eliot Ness."

"The best since him," she said. "Tell me, Nessie, what do we do next?"

"I already talked to Dylan this morning," he said, "but I need to call him again and make sure he's hacking in to Wynter's personal computer, the one he had on the yacht. Levine seemed way too interested in whether you'd managed a download."

She was pleased that she'd picked up the same nosy, untrustworthy attitude. "Something told me I shouldn't share information with him."

"Good instinct, Emily."

"Thanks."

He didn't allow her time to revel in his compliment. "We also need to talk to your friend Jerome Strauss. I'm not buying that coincidental escape from the bomb."

"Me, neither," she said. "But if he knew about the bomb, why would he stay close enough to be injured?"

"His injury makes a good alibi."

So true. The bomb almost killed him; therefore, he didn't set the bomb. She wanted to ask him why. What was his motivation for risking his life? "First we need disguises. Can we please go by my apartment? I'll only take a minute."

"We had this conversation last night."

"And I agreed that we shouldn't stay there. But a quick visit won't be a problem."

"Unless Wynter has men stationed on the street outside, watching to see if you return to your nest."

"They'd never notice me. I have a secret entrance."

HER APARTMENT WAS on the second floor of a three-story building that mimicked the style of the Victorian "painted ladies" with gingerbread trim in bright blue and dark purple and salmon pink. Following her directions, Sean drove the rental car up the street outside her home.

"Nice," he said. "You've got to be paying a fortune for this place."

"Not as much as you'd think," she said. "One of my former professors at Berkeley owns the property and makes special deals for people she wants to encourage, artists and writers."

"Wouldn't she rather have you writing poetry?"

"She likes that I do investigative journalism. It's her opinion that more women should be involved in hard-boiled reportage." She shrugged. "Otherwise, how will idealism survive?"

"Hard-boiled and idealistic? Those two things seem to contradict, but you make them fit together." He glanced over at her. "You're a dewy-eyed innocent…but edgy. That's what makes you so amazing."

Another compliment? He'd already noticed the

cleverness of her gut instincts, and now he liked her attitude. He'd called her amazing. "Turn at the corner and circle around the block so we'll be behind my building."

"Your secret entrance isn't something as simple as a back door, is it?"

"Wait and see."

The secret wasn't all that spectacular. It had been discovered by one of the other women who lived in the building, an artist. She'd been trying to evade a guy who'd given her a ride home. He wanted to come up to her place and wouldn't take no for an answer. She said goodbye and disappeared through the secret entrance.

On the block behind Emily's apartment, she told him to park anywhere on the street. She hadn't noticed anybody hanging around, watching her building. But it was better to be cautious.

As soon as she got inside, she intended to grab as many clothes and shoes as she could. Living out of one suitcase that had been packed for snow country didn't work for her.

She led him along a narrow path between a house and another apartment building. The backyards were strips of green dotted with rock gardens, gazebos and pergolas. People who lived here landscaped like crazy, needing to bring nature into their environment.

Her building had three floors going up and a garden level below. A wide center staircase opened onto the first floor. Underneath, behind a decorative iron fence, was a sidewalk that stretched the length of the building. She hopped over the fence, lowered herself to the sidewalk and ducked so she couldn't be seen from the street. There were three doors on each side for the garden-level apartments. She opened an unmarked seventh door in the middle, directly below and hidden by the staircase leading upward.

She and Sean entered a dark room where rakes and paint cans and outdoor supplies were stored. She turned on the bare lightbulb dangling from the ceiling. "In case somebody saw us, you might want to drag something over to block the door."

He did as she said. "And how do we get out?"

"Over here." She'd found a flashlight, which she turned on when she clicked off the bulb. They went from the outdoor storage room to an indoor janitor's closet with a door that opened onto a hallway in the garden level. She turned off the flashlight and put it back.

The sneaking around had pumped up her excitement. She ran lightly down the hall and up two staircases to her floor. Her apartment was on the northeastern end of the building. She wasn't an artist and therefore didn't care if she had the southern or western light.

As she fitted her key in the lock, she realized that she was excited for Sean to see her place.

When they were married, they had enjoyed furnishing their home, choosing colors and styles. For her place, she'd chosen an eclectic style with Scandinavian furniture and an antique lamp and a chandelier. Her office was perfectly, almost obsessively, organized.

The moment she opened the door, she knew something was wrong. Her apartment had been tidy before she left for Colorado. Now it was a total disaster.

Ransacked!

The sofa and coffee table were overturned. Pillows were slashed open and the stuffing pulled out. The television screen was cracked. All the shelves had been emptied.

"No," she whispered.

In her office, the chaos was worse. Papers were wadded up and strewn all across the floor and desktop. Every drawer hung open. All her articles were reduced to rubble. *Why?* What were they doing in here? Were they searching?

Barely conscious of where she was going, she stumbled into the bedroom. If they were searching, there was no need for them to go through her clothing. But her closet had been emptied and the contents of her drawers dumped onto the carpet.

Numbly, she stumbled back to the living room. On the floor at her feet was a framed photo that had hung on the wall, a wedding picture of her and Sean. She was so pretty in her long white gown with her hair spilling down her back all the way to her waist. And he was so handsome and strong. She had always thought the photo captured the true sense of romance. Their marriage didn't work, but they had experienced a great love.

The glass on the front of the photo was shattered.

Sean waved to her, signaled her. "Emily, hurry—we need to get out of here."

She heard heavy footsteps climbing the staircase outside her apartment. Her door crashed open, and she gave a yelp.

It was one of the men she'd seen with Frankie on the yacht when the murder was committed. She knew him from mug shots she'd studied when trying to identify Patrone.

"Barclay."

She knew he was a thug, convicted of assault and acquitted of murder. Not a person she'd want to meet in a dark alley.

Chapter Fourteen

The man who stormed into her apartment didn't turn around. He had his back to Sean, and he paused, staring at Emily.

This would have been an excellent occasion to use a stun gun. Sean didn't want to kill the guy, but Barclay—Emily had called him Barclay—had to be stopped.

"How do you know me?" Barclay demanded.

"I'm a reporter. I know lots of stuff." Emily hurled the framed photo at him. "Get away from me."

When Barclay put up an arm to block the frame, Sean saw the gun in his right hand. In a skilled move, he grasped Barclay's gun hand and applied pressure to the wrist, causing him to drop his weapon.

Barclay, who was quite a bit heavier and at least eight inches shorter than Sean, swung wildly with his left hand. Sean ducked the blow but caught Barclay's left arm, spun him around and tossed him onto the floor on his back. He flipped Barclay to his belly and squatted on the man's back.

Sean glanced up at Emily. "I really need to start carrying handcuffs. This is the second time in as many days that a pair of cuffs would have been useful."

Barclay squirmed below him. "Let me up, damn it. You don't know who you're dealing with."

"I know exactly who you are," Emily said. Her face was red with anger. "You were with Frankie when he shot Patrone."

"How the hell would you know about that?"

"I was there."

"No way." Though Sean had immobilized him, Barclay twisted around, struggling to get free. "Nobody was anywhere near. Nobody saw what happened."

She kept her distance but went down on her knees so she could stare into his eyes. "Three of you dragged Patrone into the office. You took turns slapping him around and calling him a coward, a term that more accurately should have been applied to you three bullies. You threw him in the chair behind the desk. Frankie screwed a silencer onto his gun and shot Patrone in the chest, twice."

Barclay mumbled a string of curses. "This is

impossible. We were alone. I swore there was no witness."

"You misspoke," she said.

"Don't matter," he growled. "It's your word against ours."

From his years in the FBI, Sean knew Barclay's assessment was true. A hotshot lawyer could turn everything around and make Emily look like a crackpot. Still, he wished she hadn't blurted out the whole story and confirmed that she was a witness. She would have been safer if there had been doubt. "Emily, pick up his gun please."

Barclay twisted his head to look up at her. "You cut your hair. I wouldn't have recognized you."

But now he would. Now he'd tell the others and they'd know exactly what to look for. Sean bent Barclay's right arm at an unnatural angle. "Why are you coming after her? What do you want from her?"

"You're hurting me."

"That's the idea." But he loosened his hold. If he hoped to get any useful information from this moron, he needed to get him talking, answering simple questions. "Have you got a first name?"

"I don't have to tell you."

Sean cranked up the pressure on his arm. "I like to know who I'm talking to."

"They call me Bulldog."

Sean could see the resemblance in the droopy eyes and jowls. "Do you know Morelli?"

"Yeah, I know him."

"Do you have a partner?"

"I work alone."

Bulldog hesitated just long enough for Sean to doubt him. He twisted the arm. "Your partner, is he waiting in the car?"

"I'm alone, damn you."

Sean decided to take advantage of this moment of cooperation. "You were told to be on the look-out for Ms. Peterson, is that right?"

"Yeah, yeah. Let go of my arm."

Sean wanted to know if Bulldog was responding to an alert that might have come from Levine or if he'd seen them sneak through her secret entrance. "Why did you come into the apartment?"

"I saw you."

"Outside?"

"No," Bulldog said. "There are two cameras in here."

Surely someone else was watching, and Bulldog would have reinforcements in a matter of minutes. They needed to get the hell out of there.

Sean should have guessed. Dylan would have figured out the camera surveillance and also would have known how to disarm the electronics. But Dylan wasn't here. Sean needed to step up his game.

"They told you to look for her," Sean said.

"When you found her, what were you supposed to do?"

"Not supposed to kill her. Just to grab her, bring her to Morelli or to Wynter."

"What do they want from her?"

"How the hell would I know?"

Sean thought back to his conversation with Morelli, who had also denied that he meant to hurt Emily. Morelli wanted information about a theft. Why did these guys think she knew something about treachery among smugglers?

Using cord from the blinds, he tied Bulldog's wrists and ankles. He could have called the FBI, but he didn't trust Levine. And they couldn't wait around for the cops; Bulldog's backup would get here first. When he pulled Emily out the door, he was surprised to see that she was dragging an extra-large suitcase.

"What's in there?" he asked.

"I'm not sure. I just grabbed clothes and shoes."

Behind the building, she struggled to push the suitcase through the grass. He took it from her and zipped across the backyards to the sidewalk to their rental car.

Using every evasive driving technique he'd been taught and some he'd invented himself, he maneuvered the rental car through the neighborhoods, up and down the hills of San Francisco on their way back to the Pendragon. Sean was good at getting rid of anyone who might be following. Sometimes he pretended he was being tailed just for the practice.

He seemed to be dusting off many of the skills he'd learned at Quantico and in the field. The martial arts techniques he'd used to take down Bulldog came naturally. And he had a natural talent for interrogation.

Still, he didn't have the answer to several questions: Why did Wynter's men think Emily knew who was stealing from them? Were they being robbed? Was it a rival gang?

It was clear to him that he and Emily needed a different approach to their situation. A strong defense was the first priority, protecting her from thugs like Bulldog who wanted to hurt her. But they also ought to develop an offensive effort, tracking down the details of the crime. He couldn't help thinking that Patrone's murder was somehow connected to the smuggling.

"I don't get it," she said. Her rage had begun to abate, but her color was still high and her eyes flashed like angry beacons. "Why did they tear my home apart? What were they looking for?"

"Evidence," he said. "The research and interviews that went into your articles about Wynter must have hit too close to home. Morelli said he wanted information from you."

"What does that have to do with my personal belongings?"

"Flash drives," he said.

"What about them?"

Her outrage about having her apartment wrecked and her things violated seemed to be clouding her brain function. "Think about it," he said. "You'd store evidence on a flash drive, right?"

"And they were searching for those." She did an eye roll that made her look like a teenager. "As if I'm that stupid? I'd never leave valuable info lying around."

She leaned back against the passenger seat and cast a dark, moody gaze through the windshield. He doubted that she even noticed that they were driving along the Embarcadero where they used to go jogging past the Ferry Building clock tower. They'd stop by the fat palm trees out in front and kiss. She'd have her long hair tamed in braids and would be dressed in layers of many colors with tights and socks and shorts and sweats. He'd called her Raggedy Ann.

Long ago, when they'd been falling in love, the scenery had felt more beautiful. The Bay Bridge spanning to Yerba Buena Island seemed majestic. He came to think of that bridge as the gateway separating him from her apartment in Oakland. When he drove across, he'd tried to leave his FBI undercover identity behind.

After swinging through a few more illogical turns, he doubled back toward Ghirardelli Square. "Do you want to stop for chocolate?"

"No," she said glumly. "Wait a minute. Yes, I want to stop." She threw her hands up. "I don't know."

"Still upset," he said. "You were pretty mad back at your apartment."

"I was."

"It showed in the way you threw that picture at Bulldog. For a minute, I thought I'd need to protect him from you."

She chuckled, but her amusement faded fast. Her tone was completely serious as she said, "I need to be able to protect myself."

"I've been thinking the same thing, but I'd rather not give you a firearm."

"Why not?" She immediately took offense. "I know how to handle a gun."

"Too well," he said. "I'd rather not leave a trail of dead bodies in our wake like a Quentin Tarantino film. I think you should have a stun gun."

"Yes, please."

At the hotel, he used the parking structure to hide their vehicle. In their suite, he ran another sweep for bugs and found nothing alarming. He might be overcautious, but it was better to be too safe than to be too sorry.

He sank down on the sofa. "I wish I'd caught the mini-cameras at your apartment. As soon as we walked in the door and saw the place ransacked, I should have known. Electronics are an easier way to do surveillance than a stakeout."

"No harm done." She flopped down beside him, stretched out her legs and propped her heels against the coffee table.

"Now they know what we look like. You heard what Bulldog said. He must have been working off an old photo of you, didn't even know you'd cut your hair."

"And they have a video of you." She smiled up at him. "Not that it matters. They already had photos of you from our wedding pictures."

"You don't keep those lying around, do you?"

"The picture I threw was from our wedding. We were outside my parents' house by the Russian olive tree."

He was surprised that she'd had their photo matted and framed and hanging on the wall. He'd stuffed his copies of their wedding photos into the bottom of a drawer. He didn't want to be reminded of how happy they'd been. "Why did you keep it?"

"Sentimental reasons," she said. "I like to remember the good stuff, like when you kissed me in the middle of the ceremony, even though you weren't supposed to."

"Couldn't help it," he mumbled. "You were too beautiful."

"What woman doesn't want a memento of the sweetest, loveliest day of her life?"

"I guess men see things differently." He slipped

his arm around her shoulders and pulled her closer until she was leaning against him.

"How different?"

"If it's over, move on," he said. "Better to forget when you've lost that loving feeling and it's gone, gone, gone. Whoa, whoa, whoa."

Her chin tilted upward. The shimmer in her lovely eyes was just like their wedding when he couldn't hold back. Sean had to kiss her. He had to taste those warm pink lips and feel the silky softness of her hair as the strands sifted through his fingers.

When he brought her back to the Pendragon, he hadn't planned to sweep her off her feet and into the bedroom, but he couldn't help himself. And she didn't appear to be objecting.

After the kiss subsided, her arms twined around his neck. She burrowed against his chest, and she purred like a feminine, feline motorboat. He rose from the sofa, lifting her, and carried her toward the bed with covers still askew after last night's tryst.

The other bed had barely been touched. The geometrically patterned spread in shades of black, white and gray was tucked under the pillows. He placed her on that bed. Her curvy body made an interesting artistic contrast with the sleek design. He could have studied her for hours in many different poses.

But she wouldn't hold still for that. "Don't we have a lot of other things to do?"

He stretched out beside her. "Nothing that can't wait."

"You haven't forgotten the murder, have you? And our investigation?"

The only detective work he wanted to do was finding out whether she preferred kisses on her neck or love bites on her earlobe. He pinned her on the bed with his leg straddling her lower body and his arm reaching across to hold her wrist. Taking his time, he kissed her thoroughly and deeply.

When he gazed once again into her eyes, her pupils were unfocused. The corners of her mouth lifted in a contented smile. But she didn't offer words of encouragement.

"This is not surrender," she said.

"We're not at war. We both want the same thing."

"Later," she whispered. "I promise."

"Don't say ground rules."

He stole a quick kiss and sprang off the bed. It took a ton of willpower to walk away from her when he so desperately wanted to fall at her knees and beg for her attention. But he managed to reach the kitchenette, where he filled a glass with water and helped himself to an apple from the complimentary fruit basket on the counter.

He was ready to get this crime solved. As soon

as he did, she'd promised to give him what he wanted. That was an effective motivation.

She appeared in the archway between the living room and bedroom. "We should start in Chinatown. And don't forget that I want to talk to Jerome Strauss."

They could launch themselves onto the city streets, trying not to be spotted by Wynter's men and hoping they'd stumble over the truth. Or they could take a few minutes to reflect and create a plan. He could use the skills he'd learned at Quantico.

"It'll save time," he said, "if we build profiles. That way, we'll know what we're looking for."

"Profiles? Like you used to do in the FBI?"

"That's right."

She'd always hated his work, and he braced for a storm of hostility. Instead of sneering, she beamed. "Let me get my computer. I want to take notes."

Her reaction was uncharacteristic. He'd expected her to object, to tell him that the feds didn't know how to do anything but lie convincingly. Instead, she hopped onto a stool and set up her laptop on the counter separating the kitchenette from the living room.

When she was plugged in and turned on, she looked up at him. "Go ahead," she said brightly. "I'm ready."

Who are you, and what have you done with

my cranky, know-it-all ex-wife? The words were on the tip of his tongue, but he knew better than to blurt them out.

She hated the FBI. While they were married, she'd told him dozens of times that he shouldn't be putting himself in danger, shouldn't be assuming undercover identities and lying to people, shouldn't be taking orders from the heartless feds. On one particularly dismal occasion, she'd told him to choose between her and his work. She would have easily won that contest, but he didn't want her to think she could make demands like that.

Her opinion had changed. And he was glad. "We need two profiles," he said, "one for the victim, Roger Patrone, and another for the person or persons who are stealing from Wynter."

"Frankie Wynter killed Patrone," she said. "What will we learn from the victim's profile?"

"We know *who* killed Patrone, but we don't know *why.* Was Frankie acting alone? Following orders from his father? It could be useful to have the victimology."

"One of the last things Patrone said before he was shot was 'I want to see the kids.' Is that important?"

He nodded. "Who are the kids, and why is he looking for them? It's all important."

While she talked, her fingers danced across the keyboard. "You mentioned profiling the person or persons who might be stealing from Wynter. Why?"

"Once we've identified them, we can use that information as leverage with Morelli and Wynter."

"Got it," she said. "Leverage."

He enjoyed the give-and-take between them. "Solving the crime against the criminals gives us something else to pass on to the FBI."

"If this all works out, we could put Wynter out of business and the person or persons who are stealing from him. We could take down two big, bad birds with one investigation." She hesitated. "It's funny, isn't it? When I look at it this way, I'm not really in danger."

"How do you figure?"

"If I tell Wynter's men what they want to know, they'll owe me a favor. At the very least, they'll call off the chase."

Her starry-eyed, poetic attitude had returned full force. Sean knew this version of Emily; he'd married her. He remembered how she'd tell him—with a completely straight face—that all people were essentially good. She was sweet, innocent and completely misguided.

He gently stroked her cheek. "I guess it's safe to say that investigative reporting hasn't tarnished your sunny outlook."

"But it has," she said. "I'm aware of a dark

side. Wynter and his crew have committed heinous crimes. They're terrible people."

"Not people you can trust," he pointed out.

"Oh."

"And what do you think these heinous people will do when they find out what you know? They'll have no further use for Emily Peterson."

"And they'll let me go," she said hopefully.

"They'll kill you."

Chapter Fifteen

Perched on a high stool, Emily folded her arms on the countertop that separated the kitchenette from the living room. She rested her forehead on her arms and stared down her nose at the flecks of silver in the polished black marble surface. She tried to sort through the options. Every logical path led to the same place: her death. There had to be another way. But what? According to Sean, Wynter's men would consider her expendable after she named the person who was stealing from them, which was information she didn't have.

"If I ever figure out who's messing with Wynter," she said, "I can't tell."

"True," Sean said. "But we've got to pretend that you know, starting now."

Crazy complicated! "Why?"

"Information is power. Wynter won't hurt us

as long as we have something he wants, either intelligence or, better yet, evidence."

"But I don't," she said.

"It's okay, as long as he doesn't know that you don't know what he wants to know."

Groaning, she lifted her head and rubbed her forehead as though she could erase the confusion. "I don't get it."

"Think of a poker game," he said. "I know you're familiar with five-card stud because I vividly remember the night you hustled me and three other FBI agents."

She remembered, too. "I won fifty-two dollars and forty-five cents."

"Cute," he said.

"I know."

"Anyway, when it comes to Wynter and the info he wants, we're playing a bluff…until we have the whole thing figured out."

"And then what happens?"

"We pull in the feds, and you go into protective custody."

"Or to Paris," she said. That was another solution. *Why not?* They could forget the whole damn thing and soar off into the sunset. "We could have a nice, long trip. Just you and me."

He still hadn't shaved off his stubble, and his black hair was tousled. He looked rather rakish, like a pirate. She wouldn't mind being looted and plundered by Sean. It wouldn't be like they were married or anything…just a fling.

"Havana," he said, "the trade winds, the tropical heat, the waves lapping against the seawall."

"Let's go right now. I could do articles about Cuba and see Hemingway's house. We'd lie in the sun and sip mojitos."

But she knew it wasn't possible to toss aside her responsibilities. She needed to take care of the threat from Wynter before he went after her family. Or her friends, she thought of the explosion at *BP Reporter*. She'd tried to call Jerome Strauss, but he didn't answer and she really couldn't leave a text or a number that could be backtracked to her.

"It might take a long time to neutralize the threat," he said. "What if it's never safe for you in San Francisco?"

"I wouldn't mind traveling the world." Living the life of a Gypsy held a certain romantic appeal. "Or I could settle down and live in the mountains with Aunt Hazel. The great thing about freelance writing is that I can do it anywhere. I might even move back to Denver."

"The city's booming," he said.

"I know. You showed me."

Looking up at him, she saw the invitation in his eyes. If she came to Denver, that would be all right with him. And she wouldn't mind, not a bit. She wanted to spend more time with him. Nothing serious, of course.

"Before I forget…" Sean went to his bag. He tucked away the device he'd used to sweep the room and took out a small, metallic flashlight. "This is for you."

"Not sure why I need a flashlight."

"This baby puts out forty-five million volts."

He held it up to illustrate. With the flashlight beam directed at the ceiling, he hit the button. There was a loud crack and a ferocious buzz. Jagged blue electricity arced between two poles at the end. A stun gun!

Eagerly, she reached for it. "I can't imagine why I haven't gotten one of these before."

"When you're testing, only zap for one second or it'll wear itself out. When you're using it for protection, hold the electric end against the subject for four or five seconds while pushing down on the button. That ought to be enough to slow them down."

"What if I wanted to disable an attacker?" Hopping down from the stool, she held the flashlight like a fencing sword and lunged forward. "How long do I press down to do serious damage?"

"Kind of missing the point," he said. "A stun gun or, in this case, a stun flashlight is supposed to momentarily incapacitate an attacker. Much like pepper spray or Mace."

"Does it hurt the attacker more if I press longer?"

"That's right," he said. "And the place on the body where you hit him makes a difference. The chin or the cheek has more impact."

"Or the groin." That was her target. A five-second zap in the groin might be worse than a bullet.

She released the safety, aimed the flashlight beam at the coffeemaker and hit the button for one second. The loud zap and sizzle were extremely satisfying. She glanced at him over her shoulder. "I'd love to try it out on a real live subject."

"Forget it."

She hadn't really thought he'd let her zap him, and she didn't want to hurt him. She hooked the flashlight onto her belt where she could easily detach it if necessary. "Have you got other weapons for me?"

"A canister of pepper spray."

"I'll take it. Then I can attack two-handed. Zap with the flashlight and spritz with the pepper spray."

"A spritz?" He placed a small container on the counter beside her computer. "Enough with the equipment. We can get started by profiling Patrone."

She climbed back up on the stool. "I've already done research on him."

"You told me," he said. "He was thirty-five, never married, lost both parents when he was nine and was raised by a family in Chinatown. Convicted of fraud, he spent three years in jail, which wasn't enough to make him go straight. He runs a small, illegal gambling operation at a strip club near Chinatown. Do you have a picture of him?"

She plugged a flash drive into her laptop and scanned the files until she located Roger Patrone. The photo she had was his booking picture from when he was recently arrested. A pleasant-looking man with wide-set eyes and a flat nose, he had on a suit with the tie neatly in place. His brown hair was combed. Smiling, he looked like he was posing for a corporate ID photo.

"For a guy who's going to spend the night in the slammer, he doesn't seem too upset," she said. "Does that attitude come from cockiness? Thinking he's smarter than the cops?"

"Maybe," Sean said as he squinted at the picture. "Does he strike you as being narcissistic?"

"Not really. To tell the truth, I feel sorry for him. He's kind of a lonely guy. Doesn't have much social life and never married. Apart from Liane Zhou, I couldn't find a girlfriend. I only talked to one woman at the strip club, and she said he was a nice guy, always willing to help her out. In other words, Patrone was a pushover."

"Characteristic of low self-esteem, he's easily manipulated," Sean said. "But why is he smiling in his booking photo?"

"It's a mask," she said. "When life is too awful to bear, Patrone puts on a mask and pretends that everything is fine."

When she looked over at Sean, he nodded. "Keep going."

"He ignored trouble while it got closer and closer. When he finally took a stand, it got him killed."

"That's a possible scenario," he said. "You're good at reading below the surface."

A thrill went through her. It was comparable to the excitement she experienced when she'd written a fierce and beautiful line of poetry. "Is this profiling?"

"Basically."

"I like it."

"We're using broad strokes," he said. "Our purpose is to create a sketch. Then we'll have an idea of what we should be looking for to fill in the picture."

"Can I try another direction?" she asked.

"Go for it."

"Abandonment issues." She pounced on the words. "His parents left him when he was only nine. And he probably didn't fit in very well with the kids in Chinatown. He didn't know the customs, didn't even speak the language."

"Feelings of abandonment might explain why he joined Wynter. Patrone needed a place to belong, a surrogate family."

"Frankie was like a brother. Patrone trusted him, believed in him," she said. "And Frankie shot him dead."

What had Patrone done to deserve that cruel fate? The Wynter organization was his family, and yet there was something so important that he betrayed them.

Sean echoed her thought. "What motivated Patrone to go against people he considered family?"

"He mentioned seeing the children, which makes me think of human trafficking."

"No doubt," he said. "The theft Morelli mentioned might be about smuggling. Wynter's best profits come from shipping people, mostly women and children, in containers from Asia."

"Someone is stealing these poor souls who have already been stolen." Disgust left a rotten taste in the back of her mouth. "There's got to be a special place in hell for those who traffic in slavery."

"You're passionate about this. I could feel it when I read the series of articles you wrote on the topic."

She was pleased that he'd read the articles, but she wished he hadn't noticed her opinion. "Those were supposed to be straightforward journalism, not opinion pieces."

"You successfully walked that line," he said. "Because I know you, I could hear the rage in your voice that you were trying so hard to suppress. Most people feel the way you do."

"Which is still not an excuse to rant or editorialize," she said. "Anyway, I think we know what was stolen...people."

"Bringing us to our second profile, namely, figuring out who's stealing from Wynter. What are the important points from your research?"

She didn't need to refer to a computer file to remember. "Trafficking is a thirty-two-billion—that's billion with a *b*—dollar business. It's global. Over twelve million people are used in forced labor. Prostitution is over eight times that many. Those are big numbers, right?"

He nodded.

"Less than two thousand cases of human trafficking ended in convictions last year."

She could go on and on, quoting statistics and repeating stories of sorrow and tragedy about twelve-year-old girls turned out on the street to solicit and seven-year-old children working sixteen-hour days in factories.

After a resigned shake of her head, she continued. "Here's the bottom line. Wynter probably imports around a thousand people a year and scoops up three times that many off the streets.

His organization has never once been successfully prosecuted for human trafficking. Mostly,
this is because the victims are afraid to accuse
or testify."

He sat on a stool beside her at the counter.
"Much as I hate to be the optimistic one, I'm
thinking it's possible that the person who stole
from Wynter had a noble motive."

"Free the victims?" She gave a short, humor-
less laugh. "That's unrealistic, painfully so. The
trafficking business runs on fear and brutality.
These people are too terrified to escape. They've
seen what happens to those who disobey."

When she first dug into the research on Wynter, she'd considered breaking the first rule of
journalism about not getting involved with your
subject. She'd wanted to sneak down to the piers,
wait for a container to arrive and free the people inside. Her fantasy ended there because she
didn't know what she'd do with these frightened
people. They'd been stolen and dumped in a land
where they knew no one and nothing.

"Impossible," she muttered.

"Not really."

"Even with noble motives, it'd be extremely
hard to do the right thing."

"Rescuing the victims couldn't be a one-
person operation. You'd need transportation,
translators, lawyers and more. The FBI would
coordinate." He paused to put the pieces together.

"I'm sure they aren't involved in anything like this at present. If they had a rescue strategy under way, you can bet that Levine would have bragged to us about it."

Another thought occurred to her. "What if it wasn't a hundred people being stolen from Wynter? What if it was only a handful of kids?"

He jumped on her bandwagon. "A few kids could be separated from the others by an inside man, someone like Patrone."

She built on the theme. "He could have been helping someone else, maybe doing a favor for the woman who raised him. Or it could have been Liane."

She wanted to believe this was what had happened. Patrone had been trying to do a good thing. He didn't die in vain. He was a hero.

"More likely," Sean said, "the human cargo was stolen by a rival gang."

"Who'd dare?" From the little she knew about the gangs in San Francisco, they focused on local crime, small scale. "Wynter is big business, international business."

"So are the snakeheads."

And they were lethal. "Liane's brother is a snakehead."

"Her brother might have used Patrone to get access to the shipments. He could have told them arrival times and locations."

"And Frankie found out."

She shuddered, imagining a terrible scenario with Patrone caught between the brutal thugs who worked for Wynter and the hissing snake-heads.

Which way would he go? Being shot in the chest was a kinder death than what the snake-heads would do to him. She hoped that was a decision she never had to make.

Chapter Sixteen

While tracking down Jerome Strauss, Emily insisted on taking the lead. She was driving when they went down the street where the *BP Reporter*'s offices had been. The storefront windows were blown out, and yellow crime scene tape crossed off the door. The devastation worried her. "If Jerome had been in there, he would have been fried."

In the passenger seat, Sean held up his phone and snapped photos. "I'll send these pictures to Dylan. He might be able to give us a better idea of what kind of bomb was used."

"I'll circle the block again."

She wasn't sure how the attack on Jerome connected to her. He knew her as Emily, a poet who he occasionally published in the *Reporter*. Her journalism was done under a pseudonym. She'd engineered the publication of the Wynter material by Jerome, making sure he got it for free.

And they'd discussed the content. But she never claimed authorship.

She thought of Jerome as a friend. Not a close friend or someone she'd trust with deep secrets but somebody she could have a drink with or talk to. She'd hate if anything bad happened to him, and it would be horrible if the bomb had been her fault.

On this leg of their investigation, she and Sean were more prepared for violence. She had her pepper spray spritzer and stun gun. He was packing two handguns, two knives, handcuffs, plastic ties to use as handcuffs, mini-cameras and other electronic devices. Sean was a walking arsenal, not that he looked unusual, not in the least. His equipment fit neatly to his body, like a sexy Mr. Gadget. Under his olive cargo pants and the denim jacket lined with bulletproof material, he wore holsters and sheaths and utility belts.

Her outfit was simple: sneakers and skinny jeans with a loose-fitting blouse under a beige vest with pockets that reminded her of the kind of gear her dad used to wear when he went fishing in the mountains. This vest, however, was constructed of some kind of bulletproof Kevlar. She also wore cat's eye sunglasses and a short, fluffy blond wig to conceal her identity.

Sean's only nod to disguise was slumping and pulling a red John Deere baseball cap low on his forehead. Surprisingly, his change of appearance was effective. The slouchy posture made his toned, muscular body seem loose, sloppy and several inches shorter. He'd assumed this stance immediately; it was a look he'd developed in his years working undercover.

Years ago, she'd hated when he left on one of those assignments. The danger was 24/7. If he made one little slip, he'd be found out. While the life-threatening aspect of his work had been her number one objection, she'd also hated that he was out of communication with her or anybody else. She'd missed him desperately. He'd been her husband, damn it. His place had been at home, standing by her side. To top it off, when he finally came home, he couldn't tell her what he'd done.

Given those circumstances, she was amazed that their marriage had lasted even as long as it did.

At the crest of a steep hill, she cranked the steering wheel and whipped a sharp left turn while Sean crouched in the passenger seat beside her, watching for a tail.

"Are we okay?" she asked.

"I think so. Are you sure you don't want me to drive?"

"I've got this."

Actually, she wasn't so sure that she could find Jerome's apartment. The only time she'd visited him had been at night, and she'd been angry. She wasn't sure of the location. And she didn't have an address because he was subleasing, and there was somebody else's name above his doorbell.

Also, it was entirely possible that he hadn't returned home after leaving the hospital. "I hope he's all right," she said.

"The docs wouldn't have released him if he wasn't."

It was difficult to imagine Jerome in a hospital bed with his thick beard and uncombed red hair that always made her think of a Viking. "I'm guessing that he wasn't a good patient."

"Are we near his apartment?"

"I think so."

Jerome liked to present himself as a starving author with a hip little publication. Not true. He had a beer belly, and his beard hid a double chin. Not only was he well fed but he lived in a pricey section of Russian Hill with a view of Coit Tower from his bedroom. The word *bedroom* echoed in her mind. She never should have gone into his bedroom.

In her one and only visit, she'd been naive, and he'd had way too much to drink. While showing her the view, he lunged at her. She sidestepped and he collapsed across his bed, unconscious. She left angry. Neither of them had spoken of it.

She recognized the tavern on the corner, a cute little place called the Moscow Mule. "Almost there, it's one block down."

As they approached, Sean scanned the street. "I don't see anybody on stakeout, but I'm not making the same mistake twice. Go ahead and park."

In one of the multitude of pockets in his cargo pants, he found a gray plastic rectangular device about the size of a deck of playing cards. He pulled two antennae from the top.

She parallel parked at the curb. "What's that?"

"It's a jammer. It disrupts electronic signals within a hundred yards."

"Inside Jerome's apartment," she said, "hidden cameras and bugs will be disabled."

He handed her a tiny clear plastic earpiece. "It's a two-way communicator. You can hear me and vice versa."

"But won't this little doohickey be disrupted as well?"

"Yeah," he said with a nod, "but I'll only use the jammer for three minutes while I enter Jerome's place. I'll get him out of there, and deactivate the jammer while I bring him down to the car."

Compared to dodging through the broom closet at her place, this was a high-tech operation. She popped the device in her ear. "I'm ready."

He slipped out the door, barely making a sound. Turning around in the driver's seat, she watched him as he strode toward the walk-up apartment building, staying in shadows. Though Sean was still doing his slouch and his poorly fitted denim jacket gave him extra girth, he looked good from the back with his wide shoulders and long legs. She was glad to be with him, so glad.

As he entered Jerome's building across the street from where she'd parked, she heard his voice through the ear device. "I'm in," he said. "Which floor?"

"Wow, your voice is crystal clear. Can you hear me?"

"I can hear. Which floor?"

"Jerome is three floors up, high enough to have a view, and his apartment is to the right of the staircase. I can't remember the number, but it's toward the front of the house and—"

A burst of static ended her communication. *Jammer on!*

She looked over her shoulder at the apartment building. If it had been after dark instead of midafternoon, Jerome would have turned his lights on. They would have known right away if he was home or not.

Had three minutes passed? She should have set a timer so she'd know when he'd been gone too long. Not that they'd discussed what she should do if Sean didn't return when he said he would. Her fingers coiled around the flashlight/stun gun. If thugs were hiding out in Jerome's apartment, she might actually have a chance to use it.

The static in her ear abruptly ended. She heard Sean's voice, "Jerome's not here. I'm sure it's his place. He's got stacks of *BP Reporter* lying around."

"What a jerk," she muttered. "He promised to distribute these all over town. They're free-bies, after all."

"Great apartment, though. Excellent view."

She saw Sean leave the building and jog to the car. He'd barely closed the door when she offered a suggestion. "We should try the tavern down the block. Jerome goes there a lot."

"No need for an earpiece." He held out his hand, and she gave him the plastic listening device. "Let's go to the Mule."

Sean took over the driving duties and chose his parking place so that if they ran out the back door from the Mule, the rental car would be close at hand for a speedy getaway. He wasn't sure what to expect when they entered through the front door. A tavern named Moscow Mule in the Russian Hill district was a little too cutesy for his taste, and he was glad the Mule turned out to be a reg-ular-looking bar, decorated with neon beer signs on the wall and an array of bottles. Stools lined up in a long row in front of the long, dark wood bar. The only Moscow Mule reference came from the rows of traditional copper mugs on shelves.

Jerome Strauss sat at the bar, finishing off a beer and a plate of French fries. He didn't seem to notice them, and Sean led Emily to a table near the back.

She sat and leaned toward him. "I can't believe he didn't recognize me. This blond wig isn't a great disguise."

"Maybe your friend Jerome isn't that bright."

When she chuckled, he noticed Jerome's re-action. His back stiffened, and he tilted his head as though that would sharpen his hearing. Sean wasn't surprised. You can change the tone of your voice, but it's nearly impossible to disguise a laugh.

Whatever the reason, Jerome spun around on his bar stool and stared at Emily. His big red beard parted in a grin as he picked up his beer and came toward them.

He squinted at her. "Is that you, Emily?"

"Join us," she said.

He wheeled toward Sean. "And who's this dude? Is he supposed to be your bodyguard?"

"That's right," Sean said as he rose to his full height, towering over Jerome. In case the editor wasn't completely intimidated, Sean brushed his hand against his hip to show his holstered gun. "Ms. Peterson asked you to join us."

"Sure." Jerome toppled into a chair at the table.

Emily gave Sean an amused smile. "Would you like to try a Moscow Mule?"

"Not now," he said for Jerome's benefit. "I'm on duty."

"They're really yummy, made with vodka, ginger beer and lime juice and served in one of those cute copper mugs."

Obviously she'd tasted the drink before. It was a somewhat unusual cocktail, probably not available in many places. Sean had to wonder if she'd spent much time with Jerome in this tavern. The newspaper editor had a definite crush on her.

"I like the blond hair," Jerome said.

Sean suspected that he'd like her whether she was blonde, brunette or bald. But they hadn't come here to encourage their friendship. "You don't seem curious, Mr. Strauss, about why Emily is in disguise and why she needs a bodyguard."

"I can guess." When he leaned forward, Sean noticed his eyes were unfocused. Jerome was half in the bag. He whispered, "To protect you from Wynter."

She fluttered her eyelashes. In the fluffy wig, she managed to pull off an attitude of hapless confusion. "Whatever do you mean? I'm a poet. Why would I have anything to do with a murderous thug like Wynter?"

"You can drop the act," Jerome said. "I've known for a long time that you're Terry Greene, the journalist."

She didn't bother to deny it. "How did you guess?"

"I'm an editor, a wordsmith. I noticed similarities in style. Even your poetic voice reminded me of Greene's prose. You have a way of writing that keeps the passion bubbling just under the surface."

"Uh-huh." Disbelief was written all over her face. The fluffy blonde had been replaced by cynical Emily. "Tell me how you really figured it out."

"I wasn't spying on you. It was an accident." He drained the last of his beer. "I noticed some of the Wynter research on your computer, but don't worry."

Jerome waved to the bartender, pointed to his empty bottle and held up three fingers.

"Don't worry about what?" Emily asked.

"I never told those guys, never, ever." The alcohol was catching up with him. Jerome had trouble balancing on his chair and rested his palms on the table as an anchor.

"What guys?" Emily asked. Her disbelief had turned into concern. "Did someone threaten you? Did they blow up your office?"

"Shhhhh." He waited until three beers were delivered and the bartender returned to his other customers. It was too early for the after-work crowd, but there were a half dozen other people at the bar and at tables.

Emily grasped Jerome's hand. "Tell me."

He raised her fingers to his lips and kissed her knuckles. "A guy came to talk to me. Middle-aged, expensive suit, slicked-back hair, he showed me a business card from Wynter Corp, like it was a regular legit business."

"Morelli," she said. "What did he want?"

"He asked for Terry Greene, and I told him that the Wynter article was just a reprint. He'd have to go to her original publisher." Jerome winced. "I knew it was you that he was after, and that's why I blew up my office."

"What!" She spoke so loudly that everybody in the bar paused to stare. Emily waved to them. "It's okay—nothing to worry about."

"You've got to believe me," Jerome begged. "I'd never tell."

When the murmur of conversation resumed, she glared at him. "You blew up your own office. What the hell were you thinking?"

"I was afraid I might accidentally spill something incriminating, and I didn't want to risk exposing you. Don't you see, Emily? I did it for you."

She surged to her feet and took a long glug of beer. "Please don't do me any more favors."

Sean believed that Jerome was telling the truth, but it wasn't the whole story. Something had scared him enough to make him blow up his office. He was in this bar because he was afraid to go home. And Morelli wasn't all that frightening.

"Who else?" Sean asked. "After Morelli left, who else paid you a visit?"

"I don't know what you're talking about." He lifted the beer bottle to his lips but didn't drink. "I'd never, ever tell. What makes you think there was somebody else?"

His fingers trembled so much he couldn't manage another swig of beer. Though he was half-drunk, Jerome's eyes flickered. He was lying. Sean figured that someone else had been following Morelli, wanting to know what he knew. And the second someone was menacing. "Who was it?"

"Frankie," Emily said. "Was it Frankie Wynter? I feel terrible for putting you in this position. Did he threaten you?"

"I'm the one who should feel bad."

Sean agreed. He figured that Jerome had let vital information slip to the other visitor. It was probably an accident, but Jerome had been terror stricken, numb, and in that state, he'd revealed Emily's true identity. "Was it Frankie? Or someone else?"

"A Chinese guy." Jerome stared down at the tabletop. "A snakehead."

Chapter Seventeen

Sean had been hoping to avoid confrontation with the snakeheads. They descended from gangs in Asia that had roots going back hundreds of years. He'd heard that the word *thug* had been invented to describe the snakeheads that, in ancient days, preyed on caravans. Now they specialized in grabbing people from Asian countries and transporting them around the world to North America, Australia and Europe.

After warning Jerome that he was damn right to be scared if he'd crossed the snakehead, Sean told the half-drunk editor that hiding out in the corner bar wasn't going to save him. He needed to go to the police…even if he'd been stupid enough to blow up his own office.

Then Sean swept Emily away from the bar and into their rental car. The answers to their investigation would be found in Chinatown. Sean was certain of it. But he wasn't sure how to proceed.

Taking extra care to avoid being followed, he made a couple of detours to grab something to eat. San Francisco truly was a town for food lovers. The array of fast food included sushi, fresh chowder, meat from a Brazilian steak house and the best hamburgers on earth. He stocked up and then drove back to the hotel.

As soon as she entered their room, Emily yanked the blond wig off her head and took the carryout bags from him. "I'll set up the food while you do your searching-for-bugs thing."

He placed the jammer on the small round table, pulled up the antennae and turned it on. Sean wasn't taking the smallest chance that they might be overheard. "After we eat, we're going to plan the rest of our time in San Francisco. Then we're out of here."

The corner of her mouth twisted into a scowl. "Do you mind if I ask where?"

"I'm not sure. We're going far, far away from the thugs and Wynter and all the many people who want to kill you."

"I don't understand. I'm such a nice person."

"Speaking of not-so-nice people," he said, "I'd advise you to keep your distance from Jerome. Not only is he crazy enough to set a bomb in his own office but he's a coward."

"What do you mean?"

"I think we have Jerome to thank for making the link between Emily Peterson and your pseudonym."

"But he said…" She paused. "Wasn't he telling the truth?"

"He protested too much about how he'd never tell. I call that a sure sign of a liar."

He swept the room, still finding nothing. Thus far, the hotel had been safe. But how much longer was this luck going to hold? After turning off the jammer, he sat at the table and gazed across at the fine-looking lady who had once been his wife. She liked to set a table, even if they were only eating fast food on paper plates.

Using the chopsticks that came with their order, he picked up a tidbit of sushi. In addition to the California rolls and *sashimi*, he'd ordered fried eel, *unagi*, because it was supposed to increase potency and virility. Not that he believed in that kind of magic…but it couldn't hurt.

"This meal almost makes sense," she said. "We start with the colorful orange-and-green sushi appetizer, then the hamburger and fries main course and finally the doughnuts for dessert."

"Perfect." He wasn't exaggerating. It was an unproven fact that eight out of ten American men would choose burgers and doughnuts for any given meal.

"And what do we do with the lovely hula Hawaiian pizza? And the meat and salad from the steak house?"

"We might not have another chance to eat for the rest of the day. I say we fill up."

She gave an angry huff. "I've told you a million times about how you can't eat once and expect it to last for hours. It's like fuel—you have to keep burning at a steady level."

"Spicy," he said as he assembled a piece of ginger, *wasabi* and *unagi*. "Eat what you want, and we'll take the rest with us."

"Fine." She raised the burger to her mouth. "Tell me about our next plan."

"First we make a phone call to Dylan and find out how much he's learned from hacking. After that, we go to Chinatown."

"After dark?"

He nodded. "At night, we don't stand out as much. Well, I do because I'm tall, but you can blend right in if you keep your head down. While we're there, we need to visit Doris Liu and Liane Zhou, the girlfriend."

"Whose brother is a snakehead," she reminded him. "Do you think Mikey Zhou was the guy who frightened Jerome?"

"It'd be neat and tidy if he was the one," he said.

"Otherwise, we need to start working another angle."

"I don't think so. If this scenario doesn't pan

out, we've got to move on. I'd like to resolve the motive for the murder, but it's too dangerous and too complex for us to solve."

"Is it really? Look at how much I got figured out all by myself."

"That's because you're a skilled and talented investigative journalist."

For a moment, they ate in silence. He enjoyed the stillness of late afternoon when work assignments were winding down and evening plans had not yet gotten under way. The sunlight faded and softened. The streets were calm before rush hour. It was a time for relaxing and reflecting. Though he'd seldom worked at a desk job with nine-to-five hours, his natural rhythm made a shift from work time to evening.

His gaze met hers across the table. She was alert but not too eager. In spite of her mini-lecture about his poor eating habits, she wasn't pushing that agenda. Not like when they were married, and she felt like she had to change him, to whip him into shape.

He didn't miss the nagging, but he wondered why she stopped. It must be that she'd given up on him and decided he wasn't worth all that fuss. He was just a guy she was hanging out with. Technically, he was her employee, not that he planned to charge her or Aunt Hazel for his services. He wouldn't know how to itemize a bill like that. For intimate services, should he charge by the hour or by the client's satisfaction?

"You're smiling," she said. "What are you thinking?"

"I'm imagining you in a waterfall. You're covered in body paint, wild orchids and orange blossoms, and the spray from the waterfall gradually washes you clean."

Her voice was a whisper. "Hey, mister, I'm supposed to be the poetic one."

"We've changed, both of us."

When they'd been married, she never sat still. Nor was she ever silent. He liked this new version of Emily who could be comfortable and relaxed and didn't need to fill the air with chatter.

He wiped his mouth with one of the paper napkins, came around the table and took her hands. "There's one more part to my plan that I didn't mention."

"Let me guess," she said as she stood. "It's the part that takes place in the bedroom."

Hand in hand, they walked into the adjoining room where both beds were messy. He'd hung the "Do Not Disturb" on the door and also requested no maid service at the front desk. He paused at the foot of one of the beds and turned her toward him.

He lifted her chin, gazed into her face. "Nobody ever said it had to be in the bedroom."

"That's a spa shower in the bathroom." A sly

smile curled the ends of her mouth. "I haven't figured out how to use all the spray jets."

"We can learn together."

The bathroom also used an Asian-influenced decorating theme with white tile and black accents. On the double-sink counter, there were three delicate orchids in black vases. The tub was simple and small. The shower was Godzilla. A huge space, enclosed in glass with stripes of frosted glass, the shower had an overhead nozzle the size of a dinner plate. Eight jets protruded from the wall at various heights, and there was a handheld sprayer.

He peeled off his Mr. Gadget outfit and dropped the clothes in a pile with his Glock on top for easy access. Earlier, he'd noticed a special feature in the bathroom: dimmer dials for the lights. Playing around with the overhead and four sconces around the mirrors, he set a cool, sexy mood.

"Do you like this?" he asked.

"It's almost as good as candlelight."

She didn't have nearly as many clothes as he did, but it was taking her longer to get out of them. He was happy to help, reaching behind her back to unhook her bra as she wiggled out of her skinny jeans.

He entered the shower. "I'll get the water started."

As she neatly folded her jeans, she said, "Quite

a coincidence, Sean. You have a fantasy about waterfalls, and here we are, stepping into a shower."

"Swear to God, I didn't plan this. But it's not altogether a coincidence. The thought of you, wet and naked, is real good motivation to find a shower."

With the overhead rainfall shower drizzling, he opened the door and took her hand, leading her into the glass enclosure. Her step was delicate, graceful. The dim light shone on her dusky olive skin and created wonderful, secretive shadows on her inner thighs and beneath her breasts.

When she moved under the spray and tilted her head up, he was captivated. She was everything a woman should be. How had he ever let her slip away from him?

With her back pressed into his chest, he encircled her with his arms and held her while her slick, supple body rubbed against him. The intake and exhale of their breathing mingled with the spatter of droplets in a powerful song without words or tune. Swirling clouds of steam filled the shower.

She turned on the jets and edged closer, letting the water pummel her. "That feels great, like a wet massage."

She moved him around, positioning him so he'd be hit at exactly the right place near the base of his spine. He groaned with pleasure.

They took turns soaping each other, paying particular attention to the sensitive areas and rinsing the fragrant sandalwood lather away. She massaged shampoo into her hair.

"Let me," he said, taking over the job. "I remember when we'd wash your long hair. It hung all the way down to your butt."

"A lot of work," she said.

"I like it better this way. No muss, no fuss."

"Like wham, bam, thank you, ma'am."

"Hey, there, if you're implying that I don't want to take my time, you're dead wrong. With all that hair out of the way, I can devote my attention to other parts of you."

He started by nibbling on her throat and worked his way down her body. Though he wasn't usually a fan of electronic aids, he started using the pulsating, handheld sprayer about half-way down.

The way she shimmied and twitched when aroused drove him crazy. Her excitement fed into his, building and building. One thing was clear: he wasn't going to be able to hold back much longer. On the verge of eruption, he had to get her into the bedroom. In the shower, he wasn't able to manage a condom. For half a second, he wondered if using prevention was necessary. Would it be a mistake to have a kid with Emily? He shook his head, sending droplets flying. Now was not the time for such life-changing decisions.

He brought her from the shower to the bed, tangling them both in towels. Condom in place, he entered her. Her body was ready for him, tight and trembling. She was everything to him.

An irresistible surge ripped through him. He felt something more than physical release. More than pleasure, he felt the beginning of something he'd once called love. *Not the same.* He couldn't be in love with her. Those days were over.

He collapsed on the bed beside her. They lay next to each other, staring up at the ceiling, thinking their own private thoughts. Did he love her? He'd give his life for her without a second thought. Was that love? She delighted him in so many ways. *Love?* He was proud of her, of the woman she'd become.

Does it matter? He should let those feelings go. Taking on the biggest gang in the city and the snakeheads, they'd probably be dead before the night was over.

He cleared his throat. "After Chinatown, we've done all the investigating that we can hope to do. Then we leave. We need to put distance between us and the people who want us dead."

"Right."

Reluctantly, he hauled himself up and out of the bed. "I need to make that call to my brother."

Swaddled in the white terrycloth robe provided by the hotel, he went to the desk in the living room and set up his computer equipment to have a face-to-face conversation with Dylan. Through the windows, he noticed that dusk had taken hold and the streetlights were beginning to glow. By the time he was prepared to make contact, Emily had blow-dried her hair and slipped on a nightshirt that left most of her slender, well-toned legs exposed.

She sprawled on the sofa. "Put it on speakerphone."

He took out the earbuds and turned up the volume. Though it was after eight o'clock in Denver, Dylan answered the number that rang through to the office immediately.

"Are you still at work?" Sean asked.

"Of course not. I transferred everything to a laptop, and I'm at my place."

"Turn on your screen and let me see."

"Just a sec."

Sean heard the unmistakable sound of a female voice, and he asked his brother, "Am I interrupting something?"

A slightly breathless female answered, "Hello, Sean. How's San Francisco? It's one of my favorite places. With the cable cars and the fog. Did I mention? This is me, Jayne Shackleford."

She was the neurosurgeon his brother had been dating and was crazy in love with. Sean envied the newness of their relationship. He and Emily would never have that again; they were older and wiser.

"It's a great city." He liked it better when nobody wanted to kill him and Emily. "Put Dylan on."

After a bit of fumbling around, his brother was back on the line. He turned on his screen so Sean could see into his house and also catch a glimpse of Jayne in a pretty black negligee before she flitted from the room.

"Here's the thing," Dylan said. "I've done a massive hack in to Wynter's accounts, both personal and professional. It took some special, super-complicated skills that I'm not going to explain. I'll take pity on your Luddite soul that barely comprehends email."

"Thanks."

"Is that Emily I see behind you?" Dylan leaned close to the screen and waved. "Hi, Emily."

From her position on the sofa, she waved back, "Right back at you, Dylan."

"You did good. You gathered a ton of info with the research tools at your disposal. But you were missing the key ingredient, namely, James Wynter's personal computer."

"I knew it." She straightened up. "The personal documents are what I was going after on his yacht."

"That's where he kept the real records that didn't synch up with income."

"What does it prove?" Sean asked.

"Somebody's stealing from Wynter," Dylan

said. "If I have the codes figured correctly, and I'm sure I do, he lost twelve people last month. They disappeared."

"And there's no way to track them?"

On-screen, Dylan shook his head and rolled his eyes. "What part of disappeared don't you understand? These people—referred to as human cargo—were supposed to arrive at Wynter's warehouse facility. They just didn't show."

Sean took a guess. "Did they come from Asia? Arriving in shipping containers?"

"There was a container. It came up three children short, five-year-olds. All the adult females were accounted for."

And the women would never rat out the kids if they'd somehow found a way to escape. Could those be the children whom Patrone was concerned about?

Sean asked, "What about the other nine?"

"They came on a regular boat. One way Wynter smuggles from Asia is taking his yacht out to sea, picking up the cargo and returning to shore north of San Francisco where he off-loads. Morelli was in charge of the last delivery, which was over six weeks ago."

"When Patrone was killed," Emily said.

"You guessed it," Dylan said. "No human trafficking since then. There's got to be a connection."

"What happened to the nine?" Dylan asked.

"Morelli swore they got onto a truck."

"But they disappeared," Sean said. "You don't happen to know where the yacht off-loads?"

"Medusa Rock, a little town up the coast."

Sean offered his usual brotherly, laconic compliments for a job well done. In contrast, Emily was over the moon, couldn't stop cheering.

"Enough," Dylan told her. "Sean'll get jealous. It's not good to have big brother ticked off."

"He most certainly can be a bear."

Sean growled. "If you two are done, I've got one more question for Dylan. Is Wynter connected with the snakeheads?"

"He's refusing to pay the snakeheads until he gets his hands on the missing twelve. The local gangs are up in arms, inches away from gang warfare."

And Sean and Emily were right in the middle.

Chapter Eighteen

Emily decided against the blond wig for their trip to Chinatown. Instead she tucked her hair behind her ears and put on a baseball cap. She wore high-top sneakers, jeans and a sweatshirt because it was supposed to be chilly tonight. All her curves were hidden. She looked like a boy, especially when she added the khaki bulletproof vest.

Sean regarded her critically. "Do you have a beret?"

"Not with me. I have a knit cap in cranberry red that I packed for the mountains."

"Put it on," he said.

"Really? But the baseball cap is better. I'm trying to pass for a boy."

He slung an arm around her waist, pulled her close and gave her a kiss. "There's too much of the feminine about you. You look like a girl pretending to be a boy, and that attracts attention."

She dug through her suitcase until she found the cap. It covered her ears, smashed her hair down and had a jaunty tassel on top.

"Better," he said.

"Yeah, great. Now I look like a deranged girl."

"When we're on the street," he said, "keep your head down. Don't make eye contact. If they don't notice you, they can't recognize you."

He was more intense than earlier today, and that worried her. "Who do you expect to run into?"

"We're walking into the tiger's maw."

"Very poetic."

"I stole it from you," he said, "from a poem you wrote a long time ago. The description applies. Chinatown is home base for the snakeheads and a familiar place for Wynter's men. I bet they even have a favorite restaurant."

"The Empress Pearl."

When she first started her research, she'd gone there several times to watch Wynter's men and try to overhear what they were talking about. She'd often seen Morelli, but when they finally met for his interview, he didn't recognize her, which made her think that Sean was right about being anonymous and, therefore, forgettable.

She asked, "Are we coming back to the hotel?"

"Sadly no, our suitcases are packed."

"I want to make a phone call from here to Morelli. If he tries a trace, it doesn't matter."

Thoughtfully, he rubbed his hand along his still unshaven jawline. "Why talk to him?"

"At one time, we had a rapport, and maybe that counts for something. I have a question I hope he'll answer."

"You're aware, aren't you, that Morelli is the most likely person to be stealing from Wynter? He has inside information, and he signed off on the nine that went missing."

"I think he's being framed," she said.

"We never did a profile on Morelli," he said. "I see him as a corporate climber, a yes-man scrambling to get ahead. He wouldn't take the initiative in stealing from Wynter, but he might support the double-crosser who took off with the nine."

All this crossing and double-crossing still didn't explain why they were coming after her. Like Bulldog said at her apartment, Wynter wasn't worried about her eyewitness testimony. His expensive attorneys were clever enough to make her look like the crook. If she was about to be framed, she wanted to know why.

She took her last burner phone from her pocket. "I'm making the call."

"And leave the phone behind," he said.

It took a moment to find Morelli's number. He answered quickly, and his voice had a nervous tremor. When she identified herself, he sounded like he was on the verge of tears.

"Emily, I have to meet with you, please. Name the place."

"Actually, John…" She used his given name to put them on a more equal footing. "I was looking for some information. If you help me, I might help you."

"Always the reporter," he said. "Ask me anything."

"According to you and also to Mr. Barclay, aka Bulldog, there's a rumor floating around that I know something about human cargo going missing on shipments from Asia."

"Do you?" He was overeager. If he'd been a puppy, his tail would be wagging to beat the band.

She said, "You first."

"Based on detailed information in your articles about Wynter, I suspected that you had an inside edge. When you talked about our warehouses and distribution, you knew about the supposed warehouse where we stored our human cargo."

"What do you mean 'supposed' warehouse?"

"Don't play dumb with me, Emily. You know it's just a house with mattresses in the basement."

He had it wrong. She had the number of warehouses but not all the addresses. If she'd known where they were keeping the kidnapped people, she would have informed the police.

Morelli continued. "I thought you had inside information, and Bulldog confirmed it."

"Do you always listen to Bulldog?"

"If you didn't want him to talk, you shouldn't have left him tied up in your apartment. It only took ten minutes for somebody to show up and let him go."

"Should we have killed him?"

"Not the point," Morelli said. "He told me that you witnessed the murder from inside the closet in the office."

"That's right." She wasn't sure where this was going but wanted him to keep talking.

"You were in the private office on the yacht… alone with James Wynter's private computer. You were the one who made changes on the deliveries and receipts, trying to cover up the theft."

"I hate to burst your bubble, but everybody on that ship had access."

"Not true. The office was unlocked for a short time only. Only Frankie had a key."

And she'd been unlucky enough to stumble onto the one time when she could get herself in deep trouble. She was done with this conversation. "Here's what I have for you, Morelli. I'm leaving San Francisco and never coming back. I'm gone, so you can quit chasing me. No more threats. Bye-bye."

When she ended the call, she felt an absurd burst of confidence. She dropped the cell phone like a rock star with a microphone. *Emily out.*

AFTER DARK, CHINATOWN overflowed with activity. Sean parked downhill a few blocks, avoiding the well-lit entrance through the Dragon's Gate. They hiked toward the glaring lights, the noise of many people talking in many dialects and the explosion of color. Lucky red predominated. Gold lit up the signs, some written in English and others in Chinese characters. Some of the pagoda rooftops were blue, others neon green.

Sean wasn't a fan of this sensory overload. He ducked under a fringed red lantern as he followed Emily toward the shop owned by Liane Zhou. His gut tensed. This wasn't a good place for them, wasn't safe. He wanted to take care of business and get out of town as quick as possible.

Emily stepped into an alcove beside a postcard kiosk and pulled him closer. "It's at the end of this block. I think the name of the shop is Laughing Duck, something like that. There isn't an English translation, but guess what's in the window."

"Laughing ducks."

"I think you should do the talking. I've already met Liane, and she was tight-lipped with me. You might encourage her to open up."

The only thing he wanted to ask Liane was if her snakehead brother intended to kill them. If so, Sean meant to retreat. "What did you talk to her about before?"

"I didn't know about the missing human cargo,

so I concentrated on Patrone. At that time, he was only missing, and I didn't tell her about the murder."

"And what did she say?" he asked.

"Not much." She scowled. "She might open up if you spoke Chinese. Do you know the language?"

"A little." He'd picked up a few phrases when he was working undercover. Needless to say, the people who taught him weren't Sunday school teachers. In addition to "hello" and "goodbye," he knew dozens of obscene ways to say "jerk," "dumb-ass" and "you suck."

"Liane is easy to recognize. She's five-nine and obviously likes being taller than the people who work for her because she wears high heels."

Glumly, he stared through the window into the fish market next door. A pyramid arrangement went from crabs to eels to prawns to a slithering array of fish. He hunched his shoulders and marched past the ferocious stink that spilled from the shop to the sidewalk. They entered the Laughing Duck, a colorful storefront for tourists with lots of smiling Buddhas, fans painted with cherry blossoms, parasols, pouches and statuettes for every sign of the Chinese zodiac. Since his zodiac animal was the pig, he pretty much disregarded that superstition. Emily was a sheep.

A young woman met them at the front with a wide smile. "Can I help you find anything?"

"Liane Zhou," he said as he entered the shop.

The narrow storefront was misleading. Inside, the shop extended a long way back and displayed more items. He knew from experience that Liane very likely sold illegal knockoffs of purses and shoes and other merchandise that was not meant to be seen by the general public.

Most of these shops had a dark, narrow staircase at the rear that led to second and third floor housing. An entire family, including mom, dad, kids and grandmas, might live in a two-bedroom flat. All sorts of business were conducted from these shady little cubbyholes, ranging from legitimate cleaning and repair services to selling drugs.

Emily's description of Liane was accurate. The tall, slender woman stood behind the glass-top counter near a cash register. She wore a bright blue jacket with a Mandarin collar over silky black pants and stiletto heels. Her sleek black hair was pulled up in a ponytail and fell past her shoulders. Her lips pursed. Her eyes were shuttered.

Hanging on the wall behind her were several very well-made replicas of ancient Chinese swords and shields. He knew enough of history to recognize that the Zhou dynasty was one of the most powerful, long-lived and militaristic. Liane was the daughter of warriors, a warrior herself.

It seemed real unlikely that she'd open up to

him…or to anybody else. He decided to start off with a bombshell and see if he could provoke a reaction.

He met her gaze. Sean had been told, more than once, that his eyes were as black as ebony. Hers were darker. In a voice so quiet that not even Emily would overhear, he asked, "Do you want revenge for the murder of Roger Patrone?"

She blinked once. "Yes."

Chapter Nineteen

A fierce hatred was etched into the beautiful features of Liane Zhou. Looking at her across the counter, Sean was convinced that the lady not only wanted revenge but was willing to rip the replica antique Chinese swords off the wall and do the killing herself.

Instinctively, he lifted his hand to his neck, protecting his throat from a fatal slash. He nodded toward the rear of the shop. "We should go somewhere quiet to talk."

Without hesitation, she shouted in Chinese to the young woman running the shop, and then she strode toward the back. When Liane Zhou made up her mind, she took action. It was an admirable trait...and a little bit scary.

Emily had fallen into line, walking behind him, and he wondered if Liane had noticed her. Behind the hanging curtain that separated the front from the back of the shop, Liane rested her hand on the newel post at the foot of a poorly lit staircase and looked directly at Emily. "Good evening, Terry Greene."

"Good evening to you," Emily said. "That's not my real name, you know."

"You are Emily Peterson. You were married to this man."

"I'm sorry I lied to you," Emily said as she pulled the cranberry knit cap off her head. "I thought an investigative reporter needed to go undercover and use an alias. I was wrong."

"How so?"

"There's never a valid reason to lie."

Liane Zhou turned her attention toward him. Her gaze went slowly from head to toe. "You," she said. "You are very…big."

Unsure that was a compliment, he said, "Thank you."

Liane took them to the second floor and unlocked the door to her private sitting room. Compared with the musty clutter in the rest of the building, her rooms were comfortable, warm and spotlessly clean.

When Liane clapped her hands, a heavily made-up woman who was skinny enough to be a fashion model appeared in an archway. Liane gave the order in Chinese, and the wannabe model scurried off.

Liane said, "We will have tea and discuss my revenge."

They sat opposite each other. Liane perched on a rattan throne while the two of them crowded onto a love seat. On the slatted coffee table between them were two magazines and a purple orchid.

Sean said, "You knew Roger Patrone for a long time."

"We arrived in Chinatown at the same time. Roger's parents sold him to Doris Liu."

Sean had never heard this version of the story. He knew the parents were out of the picture, but he didn't know why. They sold him? Sean mentally underlined abandonment issues in their profile analysis of Patrone.

"He was a boy with special talent," Sean said, taking care not to phrase conversation in questions. He wanted Liane to see him as an equal.

"He was smart." Her voice resonated on a wistful note. "But not always wise."

"A typical male," Emily muttered. "Why did Doris want him so much that she'd pay for him?"

"His English was very good. Written and spoken. And he picked up Chinese quickly, many dialects. He took care of her correspondence."

"It's a little odd," Emily said, "to trust a nine-year-old with that kind of sensitive work."

"Doris preferred using a child. She wanted him to depend on her for his food and shelter. She owned him, and he had no choice but to obey."

"How much?" Emily asked. "I'm curious."

"A thousand dollars. Doris didn't pay. Her boyfriend bought Patrone as a gift. How could that ugly old hag have a man?" She scowled. "Must be witchcraft, *wugu* magic."

The wannabe model brought their tea on a dark blue tray with a mosaic design in gold and silver. She gave a slight bow and left the apartment.

Though they appeared to be alone, Sean didn't trust Liane. Until he felt safer with her, he'd keep the conversation in the past, going over information that wasn't secret and held no current threat. "You didn't live with Doris Liu."

"Only when I chose to," she said. "My parents would never sell me. They were brave and good. In China, we were poor. Life was difficult. But they would not abandon me. They were killed by snakeheads who stole me and my brother."

"I'm sorry," Emily said.

"As am I."

Sean wished he could warn Emily not to blurt the truth. If she confirmed that she'd seen Frankie kill Patrone, there would be little reason for Liane to talk with them.

He sipped his tea and complimented her on the taste and the scent. "You mentioned your brother, Mikey Zhou."

"Do you know him?"

Why would he? Again Sean struggled to remain impassive. "I'm aware of him, but we've never met."

"Agent Levine said you were a good friend. Yet he has not introduced you."

Shocked and amazed, Sean swallowed his tea in a gulp. Levine had told them he had a snitch, and he'd identified that snitch as Morelli. Mikey Zhou, too? Sean's estimation of Special Agent Levine rose significantly. No wonder the guy had been slugging back vodka at breakfast. Levine was playing a dangerous game.

While he sat silently, too surprised to speak, Emily filled the empty air space.

"Greg Levine is an old friend," she said. "He came to our wedding, and we went our separate ways. You know how it is. And then Sean moved back to Colorado after the divorce."

"You made a mistake," Liane said. "You should never have let Sean go."

"Right," Emily said. "Because he's so…big."

Liane inclined her head and leaned forward. "Is it true?"

Emily looked confused. "Is what?"

"Did you witness the murder?"

Sean jumped back into the conversation with both feet. "Your brother is a snakehead. But you said the snakeheads killed your parents and abducted both of you."

"The last wish of my father was for Mikey to protect me. He did what he had to do." She exhaled a weary breath. "I was twelve, and my brother was eight. When the snakeheads took us, I knew my fate. As a virgin, I would fetch a good price for my first time. They would make me a sex worker."

Emily reached across the table and took her hand. "How did Mikey stop them?"

"He sacrificed himself. A handsome child, he could have been adopted. He might have worked as a servant. But he refused. Instead he disfigured himself. He made a long scar across his face. He was damaged goods."

"Did they hurt him?" Emily asked.

"He was beaten but not defeated. He did their bidding with the understanding that I would come to no harm. Mikey labored until he collapsed. He took on every challenge. Ultimately, the snakeheads came to respect him."

"And what happened to you?"

"The expected," she said darkly. "My flower was sold for many thousands but not enough to set me and my brother free. I wore pretty things and worked as a party girl until I was treated badly, ruined. Luckily, I had a head for numbers and learned to help Doris and others in Chinatown with accounts and contracts."

"You and Patrone worked together," Sean said.

"Patrone, my dearest friend, translated and negotiated deals with smugglers, local gangs,

Wynter Corp and snakeheads. He helped me save until I could open Laughing Duck."

While he was learning to profile, Sean had heard a lot of traumatic life stories. Few were as twisted as the childhood of Liane and Mikey… and Patrone, for that matter. No wonder Mikey Zhou had become a snakehead. And Patrone had been murdered. No doubt, Liane had secrets and crimes of her own.

"I have told my story," she said. "Now Emily must tell me. Who killed my dearest friend?"

Emily glanced at Sean. When he gave her the nod, she cleared her throat and said, "I saw Frankie Wynter and two others drag Patrone into an office on the yacht. Frankie shot him. They threw his body overboard."

Liane bolted to her feet. Her slender fingers clenched into fists at her side, and she spewed an impressive stream of Cantonese curses that Sean recognized from his undercover days.

"I promise," he said as he stood. "We'll bring Frankie Wynter to justice."

"Your justice is not punishment enough. He must die."

Sean was going to pretend that he never heard her threaten Frankie's life. The world would be a better place without the little jerk, but it wasn't his decision. And he wouldn't encourage Liane to take the law into her own hands.

"You're right, Liane." Emily also stood. "It's

not fair, and it's not enough pain. But we want to get the person who is truly responsible."

"What do you mean?"

"Frankie pulled the trigger, but he isn't very clever and certainly not much of a leader. He was probably following orders from someone higher up."

"True." Liane spat the word. "Morelli?"

"Or James Wynter himself."

"Wait!" Sean said. "We've got to investigate. We need proof that it's Morelli or Wynter or somebody else."

He glanced from one woman to the other. They couldn't have been more different. Emily had had a charmed childhood and grew up to be a poet and journalist who loved the truth. Liane had suffered; she had to fight to survive. And yet each woman burned with a similar flame. Both were outraged by the murder of Roger Patrone.

"One week," Liane said. "Then I will take my revenge against Frankie Wynter."

Sean couldn't let that happen. He feared that Liane's attack against Wynter would end in gang warfare with the snakeheads.

"We need more information," he said. "What do you know about the human cargo that's gone missing from Wynter's shipments?"

"I help these people," she said simply. "So does Mikey. If you want to speak to him, he is at the club where Patrone worked."

"How do you help them?" Sean asked.

She pivoted and stalked down a narrow hallway. Carefully, she opened the door. Light from the hall spilled across the bed where three beautiful children were sound asleep.

Liane tucked the covers snugly around them and kissed each forehead.

Chapter Twenty

On the sidewalk outside the strip club where Patrone had run an illegal poker game in the back room, Emily stared at the vertical banner that read, "Girls, Nude, Girls." The evening fog had rolled in, and the neon outlines of shapely women seemed to undulate beside the banner. A barker called out a rapid chatter about how beautiful and how naked these "girls" would be.

"Not exactly subtle," she said as she nudged Sean. "At least it's honest."

"That depends on your definition of beauty. And I'd guess that some of these ladies left girlhood behind many years ago."

"How did you get to be an expert?"

"When I was undercover, I spent a lot of time in dives like this, the places where dreams come to die." He gave her arm a squeeze. "You always wanted to know what I did on my assignments. You pushed, but I couldn't say a damn word.

The information I uncovered was FBI classified. And I felt filthy after spending a day at one of these places."

She knew his undercover work had been stressful. One of the reasons she'd pushed was so he could unburden himself. "If you'd explained to me, I would have understood. It had to be hard spending your day with addicts, strippers, pimps and criminals."

"They weren't the worst," he said. "I was. I lied to them. I knew better and didn't try to help."

"I never thought of your work that way."

"But you understand." He gazed down at her, and the glow from the pink neon reflected in his eyes. "You told Liane that you were wrong to lie when you were investigating."

"Maybe we're not so different." Why was she having this relationship epiphany on a sidewalk outside a strip club? "Let's get in there, talk to Mikey and go on our way."

He nodded. "There's not much more we can learn. I'll report to the FBI, sit back and let them do their duty."

She watched the patrons, who shuffled through the door with their heads down, looking neither to the right nor to the left. With her dopey cranberry hat pulled over her ears, she fit right in with this slightly weird, mostly anonymous herd…except for her gender. The few women on this street looked like hookers.

Inside the strip club, she pulled her arms close to her sides and jammed her hands into her pockets. The dim lighting masked the filth. The only other time she'd been here was in daylight, and she'd been appalled by the grime and grit that had accumulated in layers, creating a harsh, dull patina. Years of cigarette smoke and spilled liquor created a stench that mingled with a disgusting human odor. The music for the nude—except for G-string and pasties—girls on the runway blared through tinny speakers. Emily didn't want to think about the germs clinging to the four brass stripper poles.

Long ago, this district, the Tenderloin, had been home to speakeasies, burlesque houses and music clubs. Unlike most of the rest of the city, the Tenderloin had resisted gentrification and remained foul and sleazy.

Fear poked around the edges of her consciousness. Nothing good could happen in a place like this. She moved her stun gun from a clip on her belt to her front pocket so it would be more accessible. And she stuck to Sean like a nervous barnacle as she tried to think of something less squalid than her immediate surroundings.

Liane's life story had touched her. The woman had gone through so much tragedy, from witnessing the murder of her parents to the loss of her "dearest friend." Though she hadn't admitted that Patrone was her lover, it was obvious that she cared deeply about him. And he must have felt the same way about her. He had stolen the three children for her.

After Liane kissed the children, she explained. Patrone had been part of the crew unloading the shipping container. He'd arrived before anyone else because he was supposed to conclude negotiation with the snakeheads. When Patrone saw the kids, his heart had gone out to them. He'd unloaded them from the container and moved them to the trunk of his car. The poor little five-year-olds had been starving and dehydrated, barely able to move. Patrone had taken them to Liane.

This wasn't the first time she'd rescued stolen children and their mothers, protecting them from a life of servitude to women like Doris Liu. Liane fed them and nursed them. The plight of these kids wakened instincts she never thought she had. Though she was unable to bear children, she felt deep maternal stirrings.

Emily hoped that these three children would be Liane's happy ending. According to Emily's calculations, the children arrived shortly before Patrone was murdered. Only six weeks, but Liane loved them as though she'd raised them from birth.

Emily was content to let the story end there. She tugged Sean's sleeve and whispered, "We should go."

"After we check out the poker game," he said. "If Mikey isn't there, we're gone."

"Did Liane call him?"

"She said he'd know we were coming."

Behind a beaded curtain and a closed door, they were escorted into the poker game by the bartender, whom Sean had bribed with a couple of one-hundred-dollar bills. Emily didn't know Chinese, but she could tell from the bartender's tone as he introduced them that she and Sean were being described as rich and stupid, exactly the people you'd want to play poker with.

There were four tables: three for stud poker and one for Texas Hold'em. Emily narrowed her eyes to peer through the thick miasma of cigar and cigarette smoke. Almost every chair at the tables was filled. Most of the patrons were Asian, and there was only one other woman.

Sean guided her to a table and sat her down. He spoke to the others in Chinese, and they laughed. He whispered in her ear, "I said you were my little sister. They should be nice to you, but not too nice because you like to win."

"Are you leaving me here alone?"

"I'll be close. Don't eat or drink anything."

"Don't worry."

When she felt him move away from her, it took an effort for her to stay in the chair and not chase after him. The dealer looked at her and said something in Chinese. She nodded. Since she knew how the game was played, she could follow the moves of the other players without getting into trouble.

The player sitting directly to her right was an older man with thinning hair and boozy blue eyes. He spoke English and directed one condescending remark after another to her. If she hadn't been so scared, she would have told him off.

Her plan was to be as anonymous as possible. Then she was dealt a beautiful hand: a full house with kings high. Her self-preservation instinct told her to fold the hand and not attract attention to herself. But she really did like to win. She bid carefully, taking advantage of how the others at the table paid her very little regard.

While she was raking in her winnings, she looked around for Sean and spotted him by the far wall, talking to an Asian man with a shaved head. He gave her a little wave, and she felt reassured. He was keeping an eye on her.

She quickly folded the next two hands and then tried a bluff that succeeded. *Really?* Was she really holding her own with these guys? The condescending man on her right gave his seat to another, and she turned to nod. His thick black hair grew in a long Mohawk and hung down his back in a braid. His arms and what she could see of his chest were covered in tattoos. The scar that slashed across his face told her this was Mikey Zhou.

He leaned closer to her. His left hand grazed her right side, and she felt the blade he was holding. "Fold this hand and come with me."

"Yes," she said under her breath. Frantic, she scanned the room. Where had Sean disappeared to? How could he leave her here unprotected?

Though terrified, she managed to keep focus on the game. Lost it but played okay. She rose from the table, picked up her chips and allowed Mikey to escort her toward a dark door at the back of the room. His grip on her arm was tight.

He whispered, "Don't be scared."

Though she wanted to snap a response, her throat was swollen shut by fear. She could barely breathe. The fact that she was moving surprised her because her entire body was numb. She was only aware of one thing: the stun gun in her pocket. Somehow she got her fingers wrapped around it. She got the gun out of her pocket without Mikey noticing.

When he shoved her into a small room filled with boxes and lit by a single overhead bulb, she whirled. Lunging forward, she pressed the gun against his belly. She heard the electricity and felt the vibration.

Mikey shuddered. His eyes bulged, and he went down on his hands and knees.

Before she could move in to zap him again,

another man appeared from the shadows and grabbed her arms from behind. He knocked the gun from her hand.

She kept struggling, but couldn't break free. When she tried to kick backward with her legs, he swept her feet out from under her, and she was on her knees with her arms twisted back painfully. She tried to inhale enough air to scream. Could she summon help? Who would come to her aid? Nobody in this club was going to cross Mikey Zhou.

He stood before her and leaned down. His long braid fell over his shoulder. Roughly, he yanked her chin upward so she had to look into his dark eyes. Even with the tattoos and the scar, she saw a resemblance to Liane in the firm set of the jaw.

"Emily," he said. "Special Agent Levine said you would cause trouble."

"Let me go," she said. "I'll leave and you'll never see me again, I promise."

"I will not harm you."

He said something in Chinese to the man who was holding her arms, and he released her. She sat back on her heels. What was going to happen to her? *And where is Sean?*

If Mikey didn't intend to hurt her, why did he grab her? She wasn't out of danger, not by a long shot. "What do you want from me?"

"Wynter has an arrangement with snakeheads.

It has been thus for many years. There is disruption. Why?"

"Do you want me to find out?"

Mikey rubbed at the spot where she'd zapped him. "The disruption must end."

Slowly she got to her feet. Common sense told her that only a fool picked a fight with the snakeheads, but she didn't want to lie. The whole reason she was in trouble could be traced to her lies when she'd used an alias and posed as a hooker.

If she told Mikey that she'd help him by finding out who was messing up the smooth-running business of human trafficking, that wouldn't be the truth. She hated that the snakeheads were buying and stealing helpless people from Asia, and she also hated that Wynter Corp distributed the human cargo. Couldn't Mikey see that? After what happened to him and Liane, couldn't he understand?

She inhaled a deep breath, preparing to make her statement. These might be the last words she ever spoke. She wanted to choose them carefully.

The door whipped open, and Sean entered the room. As soon as she recognized him, he was at her side, holding her protectively.

"Are you all right?" he asked her. "Did he hurt you?"

Mikey laughed as he returned her stun gun. "Other way around."

She looked up at Sean. "He wants me to help him. I can't do that. I'm against human trafficking, and if it's interrupted, I'm glad."

"I want peace," Mikey said. "I do not hurt my own people. Explain to her, Sean."

"That might take a while."

She didn't understand what they were talking about, but it was obvious that they'd had prior contact. Did Sean know that Mikey was going to grab her and scare her out of her mind?

Mikey said, "You go now."

Sean whisked her toward the exit door from the small room. When he opened it, she saw the foggy night blowing down an alley.

"Hold on," she said, jamming her heels down. "I need to cash in my chips."

"Not tonight."

As if she'd ever return to this place? Reality hit her over the head, and she realized that she was lucky to be walking out this door with no major physical injuries.

She went along with Sean as he propelled her around the corner and down two streets to where he'd parked. A misty rain was falling, and she was wet by the time they got to the rental car. As soon as they were inside the car, he started the engine.

"We need to hurry," he said.

"Why?"

"There's another shipment coming in tonight."

She snapped on her seat belt. She had to do whatever she could, anything that would help.

Chapter Twenty-One

Mikey the snakehead would not be getting any pats on the back from Sean. After Emily told him how Mikey had mishandled her, Sean was glad she'd zapped him with her stun gun.

"He wasn't supposed to scare you," he said.

"Well, he wasn't Mr. Friendly. When he got close to me, I felt the knife in his hand."

"His comb." Mikey's long braid didn't just happen. He worked on that hair. "A metal comb."

"How was I supposed to know?" she grumbled. "All he had to do was tell me you were waiting for me. And his friend grabbed me. He twisted my arm and forced me down on my knees."

"After you zapped Mikey with a stun gun?"

"Okay, maybe I was aggressive."

"You shot forty-five million volts through him."

She huffed and frowned. "What did he mean about wanting peace?"

"I'll explain."

The fog parted as he drove toward the private marina where the Wynter yacht was moored. It was after midnight. The city wasn't silent but had quieted. Misty rain shrouded the streets.

Though Mikey was a member of the notoriously cruel and violent snakeheads, Sean was inclined to believe him. In his experience, the guys who were the most dangerous were also the most honest, flip sides of the same coin. Besides, Mikey had nothing to gain from lying to Sean.

"Mikey says he's not involved in the actual business of human trafficking. His hands aren't clean, far from it. His job is to take care of snakehead business in San Francisco, buying and selling and extracting payments. His sister's dearest friend, Patrone, helped him negotiate."

"And that's why he knows Levine," she said.

"Right. Mikey's not a snitch. He's more like a local enforcer. He knows that if the snakeheads and Wynter keep losing money, there's going to be a war."

"And we're supposed to stop it?" The tone of her voice underlined her disbelief. "I didn't sign up for this job."

It wasn't fair to drag her any deeper into this quagmire. Until now, she'd been ready to go. Mikey must have scared her, made her realize that she was in actual danger. "You're right."

"Am I?"

"I can turn this car around, hop onto I-80, and we'll be back in Colorado in two days. You'd be safer with your aunt. Better yet, TST Security has a couple of safe house arrangements."

She sat quietly, considering his offer. With a quick swipe, she pulled off the knitted cap, fluffed her hair and tucked it behind her ears. She'd been through a lot in the past few days, and Sean wouldn't blame her if she opted to turn her back on this insanity.

In a small voice, she said, "I started investigating Wynter Corp six months ago, and I've learned a lot. I want to see this through. I want justice for Patrone. And I want the bad guys punished."

Damn, he was proud of her. She'd grown into a fine woman, a fine human being. He was glad she'd chosen to stay involved. If they dragged the FBI into the picture too soon, the investigation could turn messy. Liane might lose the kids and Mikey could be in trouble. If Sean handled the things, the case would be gift wrapped and tied up with a pretty red bow.

At the marina, he parked behind a chain-link fence, grabbed a pair of binoculars and went toward the gate. Security cameras were everywhere. "We can't get much closer. Do you remember where Wynter's yacht was moored?"

"I remember every detail of that night. My red dress and the shoes I could hardly walk in. I remember the other girls, several blondes, a couple of brunettes and some Asian. And I remember Paco the Pimp. He was incredibly helpful. Sure, he charged me a hefty bribe, but he was efficient and kind. Do you think we should talk to him?"

"Save Paco for another story," he said. "Do you remember where you boarded the yacht?"

"Near the end of the pier." When she squinted through the fog, he handed over the binoculars. She fiddled with the adjustments and then lowered the glasses. "I don't see it."

"I was hoping we could catch them before they took off," he said, "but it was a long shot."

"The cargo might be arriving via container ship. We'd have to go to the docks in Oakland to check it out."

A chilly breeze swept across the bay and coiled the fog around them. He wrapped his arm around her shoulder, welcoming the gentle pressure of her body as she leaned against him. She turned, her arm circled his torso and she looked up at him.

Her cheeks were ruddy from the cold. Her eyes sparkled. Before he could stop himself, he said, "I love you."

Her lips parted to respond, but he didn't want words. He kissed her thoroughly, savoring the heat from her mouth and the warmth of her body. She felt good in his embrace, even with several layers of clothes between them.

Saying "I love you" might have been one of the biggest mistakes in his life. He might have sent her reeling backward, frantically trying to get away from his cloying touch. But he wasn't going to take back his statement. He loved her, and that was all there was to it. He'd never really stopped loving her from the first day he saw her.

When he ended the kiss, he didn't give her a chance to speak. "We need to hustle."

"Where are we going?"

"Medusa Rock."

In the car, he immediately called his brother to get the coordinates for the place where Wynter off-loaded cargo. As usual, Dylan was awake. Sean was fairly sure that his genius brother never slept. They discussed a few other electronic devices before Sean ended the call and silence flooded into the car.

After a few miles, she pointed to the device fastened to the dashboard. "Is this the GPS location?"

"That's right."

"Medusa Rock," she said. "Do you think there are a lot of snakes?"

"I don't know. It's a good distance up the coast."

Again, silence.

With a burst of energy, she turned toward him. "We had ground rules, Sean. There's no way you can tell me you love me, no way at all.

We had our chance, we had a marriage. When it fell apart, my heart shattered into a million little pieces. I can't go through that again."

"I apologize," he said. "I couldn't stop myself."

"I never thought I'd say this." When she paused, he heard a hiccup that sounded as though she was crying. "You're going to have to practice more self-control."

"Never would have believed it." He tried to put a good face on a bad move. "This time I'm the one who can't keep himself in check. I couldn't stop myself from blurting. What's the deal? Am I turning into a chick?"

"Not possible." She reached across the console and patted his upper thigh. "You're too…big."

WHEN HE TOLD her he loved her, she thought she'd explode. The longing she'd been holding inside threatened to erupt in a sky-high burst of lava. And then, to make it worse, he kissed her with one of those perfect, wonderful kisses.

They had both changed massively since the divorce, but she still wasn't ready to risk her heart in another try with Sean. Maybe she'd never be ready. Maybe they were the sort of couple who was meant to meet up every ten years, have great sex and go on their merry way.

While he drove, she kept track of their route on the GPS map. Soon this would be over, and she'd be able to use her phone again. Right now she really wanted to know about the possibility of snakes at Medusa Rock. According to the map, this place was a speck about a hundred miles north along the Pacific Coast Highway from San Francisco.

At their current speed, which was faster than she liked, they'd be there in about an hour. There was almost zero traffic on this road. In daylight when the fog burned off, the view along this highway was spectacular.

"There's a blanket in the backseat," he said. "It might be good for you to get some sleep. If we catch Wynter's men in the act, we'll need to follow them. And probably will switch off driving."

She didn't need much convincing. The spike of adrenaline from her encounter with Mikey had faded, leaving her drained of energy. She snuggled under the blanket. An hour of sleep was better than none.

It seemed like she'd barely closed her eyes when the car jolted to a stop. She sat up in the seat, blinking madly. She grasped Sean's arm. "Are we safe?"

"You're always safe with me." His voice was low and calm with just a touch of humor to let her know he was joking…kind of joking. "We're here."

"I see it." Medusa Rock sat about a hundred yards offshore. Shaped like a skull, it had shrubs and trees across the top that might have resembled snaky hair. "Looks more like Chia pet to me."

The heavy fog from San Francisco had faded to little more than a mist. The car was parked up on a hill overlooking a small marina where Wynter's party boat was moored. Sean placed the high-power binoculars in her hand, and she held them to her eyes. The running lights on the yacht were off, but there was still enough light to see four men leaning over the railing at the bow and smoking.

"How long have we been here?" she asked.

"Just a few minutes."

"They're waiting for something."

"If they take delivery from another boat," he said, "there's nothing more we can do. But if it's a truck, we'll follow."

She sat up a bit straighter in the passenger seat and fine-tuned the binoculars. The resolution with these glasses was incredible. She could make out faces and features. "Guess who's here."

"I'm pretty sure it's not big daddy James," he said. "Frankie boy?"

"The next best thing." She made a woofing noise. "It's Barclay the Bulldog, the guy who wrecked my apartment."

"It's good to know he doesn't specialize in ransacking."

"The Bulldog is an all-purpose thug." She chuckled as she continued to watch the yacht.

"If they drive, we'll be able to see where they make the drop-off."

"We'll coordinate with Levine," he said. "It's not really fair. We do all the work, and that jerk gets all the glory."

"Not necessarily," she said.

She passed the binoculars to him. A fifth man had joined the other four on deck. She'd recognized him right away from his nervous gestures. It was Special Agent Greg Levine.

Chapter Twenty-Two

Outraged, Sean stared down the hill at the fancy yacht with four thugs and a rat aboard. Levine was a double-crossing bastard who might precipitate a gang war that would tear San Francisco apart. Why hadn't Sean seen the problem before? It should have been obvious to him when he heard that Levine was using both Morelli and Mikey. *Quite a juggling act!* Levine wasn't a charmer and had nothing to offer. Neither of those men had a reason to work with him.

"Maybe," Emily said, "this is a sting."

Sean calmed enough to consider that scenario. On a scale of one to ten, he'd give it a three. Levine wasn't clever enough to set up a sting like this. And Sean hadn't noticed FBI backup in the area. Still, he conceded, "It's possible."

"But not likely," she said.

"Not at all."

They watched for another half hour. The

night was beginning to thin as the time neared four o'clock, less than two hours before sunrise. Would Levine dare to drive into San Francisco during morning rush hour? Either he was massively stupid or had balls the size of watermelons.

A midsize orange shipping truck with a green "Trail Blazer" logo rumbled down to the pier. The driver jumped out and trotted around to the back. As soon as he rolled up the rear door, the armed men on the boat herded a ragged group of people who had been belowdecks, waiting in the dark. Sean counted seventeen. Only two men; the rest were women and children. He was glad to see that they also loaded bottles of water and boxes he hoped were food.

"Now what?" she asked.

"We follow," Sean said. "As soon as we figure out his plan, we'll call for backup."

"Why wait?"

"I don't want to waste this opportunity." He was thinking like a cop, not a bodyguard, which probably wasn't a good thing. Undercover cops took risks, while bodyguards played it safe. He promised himself to back down before it got dangerous. "Their destination might lead to another illegal operation."

"Like a sweatshop," she said. "We might be

able to track the distribution network for the sex workers."

The orange truck pulled away from the pier with Levine behind the wheel and two armed men in the cab beside him. Staying a careful distance behind so they wouldn't be noticed, Sean followed in the rental car.

The roads leading away from Medusa Rock were pretty much empty before dawn. As soon as possible, Sean turned off the headlights, figuring that their nondescript sedan would be almost invisible in the predawn light.

The orange truck wasn't headed toward San Francisco. Levine was taking them east. *Where the hell is he going?*

With his assistance, Emily set up a conference call with his brother, who was—surprise, surprise—asleep. It was worth waking him up. If anybody could figure out how to track a moving vehicle, it was Dylan.

"Big orange truck?" His yawn resonated through the phone. "What do you want me to do with it?"

"We're trying to track it," Sean said. "When the sun comes up, in a couple of minutes, the driver of the truck might notice that we're tailing him. I want to drop back…way back."

"That sounds right," Dylan said. "What should I do? Turn you invisible?"

"Wake up, baby brother. I need you to be sharp now—right now."

"I have an idea," Emily said. "Satellite surveillance."

"It's hard to pull off," Dylan said. "If there are any clouds, it blocks the view."

"You could use a drone," she suggested.

"The only drones in the area are probably operated out of Fort Bragg, and I'm not going to hack in to the Department of Defense computers. Stuff like that could get me sent away for a long time."

"There must be something," she said.

"An idea," Dylan said. "Sean, do you have any of those tracking devices I put together a while back?"

"I have the big ones and the teeny-tiny ones."

"Slap a couple of each on the truck when he stops for gas. Turn them on right now, and I'll see if I can activate from here."

While they continued to follow, Sean told Emily where he kept the tracking devices in his luggage. Following his instructions, she checked batteries and made sure they were all working. She activated each.

"Good," Dylan said. "I've got four signals."

Emily chuckled. "You're amazing, Dylan. You can track us all the way from Denver?"

"And I kind of wish I could see what was

going on. In the next generation of trackers, I'm adding cameras."

"Where are we?"

"On the road to Sacramento," Dylan said. "According to my maps, there aren't any major intersections on your route."

"But he might be stopping here," Sean said as he dropped back, slowing the rental car and allowing the truck to get almost out of sight. He stretched the tense muscles in his shoulders. He didn't like keeping surveillance in crowded traffic, but these empty roads were equally difficult.

After rummaging around in his backpack, Emily found energy bars and a bottle of water. Both food and drink were welcome. He hadn't slept last night, and the sun was rising.

The orange truck rumbled through Sacramento, still heading east.

Dylan called them back with an alert. "Make sure your car has enough gas. It looks like the route he's taking is Highway 50, otherwise known as the loneliest road in America."

"That's right," Emily said. "I'm reading the road signs. It's Highway 50, and it goes to Ely, Nevada."

"The road's quiet," Sean said, "but not that lonely."

He'd actually driven Highway 50 on one of his trips between San Francisco and his parents' house in Denver. On the stretch across Nevada, there were maybe fifteen towns, some with populations under one hundred.

The good thing about the desolate road was that it wouldn't be difficult to keep track of the orange truck. The negative was that there was nowhere to hide. If he didn't stick the trackers onto the truck soon, he'd never be able to sneak up and do it.

Finally, just outside Ely, the truck made a rest stop. If Levine and the other guards had been decent human beings, they would have made sure the people in the back of the truck were okay. That didn't appear to be part of their plan.

Sean drove up a gravel road behind the gas station and parked on a hillside behind a thicket of juniper and scrub oak. With the tracking devices in his pocket, he started down the hill. Emily caught his arm.

"One kiss," she said.

They made it a quick one.

EMILY PACED BEHIND the car, stretching her legs after too many hours sitting. She needed to take her turn behind the wheel. Sean was exhausted, and she wanted to help.

Looking for a vantage point, she moved along the edge where the hill dropped off. Behind a clump of sagebrush, she crouched down and lifted the binoculars to watch Sean. He'd found a hiding place behind the gas station, not far from the orange truck.

Her heart beat faster as she realized he was in danger. He had to stay safe, had to stay in one piece. She couldn't bear to lose him again. But that was exactly what was going to happen.

She saw him dart forward and place the tracking devices, and then she lowered the binoculars. Their investigation was wrapping up. Soon, it would be over, and Sean would leave her. If they couldn't be in love, they couldn't be together. He'd be gone.

Behind her right shoulder, she heard the sound of a footstep. Someone was approaching the rental car and being none too subtle about it. She couldn't see him but as soon as she heard him wheezing from the hike up the hill, she knew it was Bulldog.

He whispered her name. "Emily. Are you here, Emily?"

What kind of game is he playing? She still had her stun gun in her pocket and wouldn't hesitate to zap him. But that meant getting close, and she preferred to keep her distance.

Again he called to her. "Come out, Emily. I have a surprise for you."

She ducked down, making sure he couldn't see her.

"Forget you," he said. "I'm outta here."

She heard him walking away and knew he'd

take the gravel road rather than scrambling up and down the hillside. She scooted around the shrubs and sagebrush to get a peek at Bulldog and see what he was doing. He jogged down the hill toward the truck. Before reaching the gas station, he paused and looked back toward the rental car.

Incongruously, he held a cell phone in his hand. With his chubby fingers, he punched in a number. The answering ring came from the rental car. That innocent sound was the trigger.

The car exploded in a fierce red-hot ball of fire.

The impact knocked her backward and she sat down hard. Her ears were ringing, and she fell back, lying flat on the dusty earth, staring up at a hazy sky streaked with black smoke from the explosion and licked with flames. The earth below her seemed to tremble with the force of a second explosion. Vaguely she thought it must be the gas tank.

Sprawled out on the ground, she was comfortable in spite of the heat from the flames and the stench of the smoke. Moving to another place might be wise. There was a lot of dry foliage. If it all caught fire, there would be a major blaze. Her grip on consciousness diminished. A soft, peaceful blackness filled her mind.

Sean was with her. He scooped her up and

carried her down the hill to the gas station. The orange truck was gone.

In the gas station office, he sat her in a chair and leaned close. "Emily, can you hear me?"

"A little."

"Do you hurt anywhere?"

She stretched and wiggled her arms and legs. Nothing was broken, but she was as stiff and sore as though she'd run a marathon. "I do hurt a little."

"Where?"

"All over." Though wobbly in the knees, she rose to her feet. She grabbed the lapels of his jacket and stared into his face. "I. Love. You."

She wasn't supposed to say that, but she meant it. If he said it back, they'd be on the same page. It would mean they should be married, again. *Say it, Sean.*

"Emily." He kissed the tip of her nose. "You need to sit down."

He guided her back into the chair, brought her cold water and a damp washrag from the restroom. Her hearing was starting to return as she watched the volunteer fire brigade charge past the gas station windows and attack the blaze.

"It was Bulldog," she said to Sean. "He set off a bomb."

"I know."

"How did he know I was with the car?"

He shrugged. "He must have spotted you

through binoculars. I was worried that they'd notice us following."

"Did you take care of the plants?"

"Mission accomplished." He ran his thumb across her lips. "You're going to be okay. I want you to stay here. I'll come back for you."

Not a chance. "This is my investigation. You're not going to leave me behind."

He didn't argue with her. As she drank her water and nibbled a sandwich the gas station owner had given her, she was aware of Sean striding around, yakking into his cell phone and making plans. If he had figured out some way to follow Levine, she was coming with him, and she told him so after he loaded her into the back of the local sheriff's car, and they went for a short ride. Had she really said, "I love you"?

As they sat in a pleasant lounge in the Ely airport, Emily's mind began to clear. She was picking up every third or fourth word as Sean buzzed around the room, talking on two phones at once. She figured, from what Sean was saying, that Dylan was able to track the orange truck. Levine wasn't getting away; he was driving into a trap.

The local sheriff and some of his deputies were in the lounge with her. Law enforcement was involved, and she was glad. She and Sean had taken enough risks. *Like saying I love you?* It was time for somebody else to step up.

Sean sat beside her. "It's almost over."

With all the excitement and confusion swirling around them, she had only one cogent thought. She loved him.

"I can't take it back," she said. "I can't lie."

"You love me," he said.

Not to be outdone, she said, "And you love me right back."

He gently kissed her, and she drifted off into a lovely semiconscious state. Still clinging to her bliss, she boarded a private plane flown by none other than their buddy David Henley. This Cessna wasn't as big or as fancy as the Gulfstream they'd taken to San Francisco, but she liked the ride.

"Sean, where are we going?"

"Aspen."

"Of course."

It made total sense. They'd gone from intense danger in San Francisco—crooked FBI agents, the crime boss's thugs and Chinese snakeheads— to the peaceful, snow-laced Rocky Mountains. She smiled. "I think we should live in Colorado."

"As you wish," he said.

"I also think I'm awake," she said. "Can you give me an explanation?"

"Dylan's tracker worked. Levine and the two idiots drove the truck on Highway 50. The feds and law enforcement are keeping tabs on them. I thought we could join in the chase at Aspen."

"Why Aspen?"

"The timing seemed right," he said. "Ely is about eight hours from Aspen."

It occurred to her that the orange truck could keep rolling all the way across the country, leading a parade of FBI agents and police officers to the Atlantic shoreline.

But that was not to be.

By the time they landed in Aspen, Sean received word that the orange truck had stopped at a ranch in a secluded clearing. The FBI was already closing in.

He turned to her. "Do you want to stay here? I could arrange for your aunt to pick you up."

"I'm coming with you. I won't let you face danger all by yourself…"

"Half the law enforcement in the western United States will be there to protect me."

"But you need me, and I need you."

"I love you, Emily."

"And I'm a reporter." She gave him a hug. "I'm not going to miss out on this exclusive story."

Sean and Emily arrived at the scene in time to see the people in the orange truck go free, as well as dozens of other women and children who had been assembling electronics at this secluded mountain sweatshop.

Greg Levine was arrested, along with the rest of the men working at the ranch and their leader. The big boss was none other than Frankie Wynter himself.

THREE WEEKS LATER, when Emily's four-part article was published, she was able to say that Frankie had been charged with the murder of Roger Patrone. Though she knew Patrone was killed because he had saved three children and thwarted Frankie's operation, she managed to write her story without mentioning the kids. Liane Zhou deserved her family.

And so did Emily. Resettling in Denver was easy. She fit very nicely into Sean's house.

On the wall by the fireplace, there were two wedding photos: one from the original wedding and another from the mountain ceremony at Hazelwood.

* * * * *

Get 2 Free Books,
Plus 2 Free Gifts—
just for trying the Reader Service!

HARLEQUIN *Presents*

Get 2 Free Books,
Plus 2 Free Gifts —
just for trying the
Reader Service!

Get 2 Free Books,
Plus 2 Free Gifts—
just for trying the Reader Service!